A CURSED MIDLIFE

WITCHING AFTER FORTY, BOOK 2

LIA DAVIS

L.A. BORUFF

D1526379

A Cursed Midlife

© Copyright 2021 Lia Davis & L.A. Boruff

Published by Davis Raynes Publishing

PO Box 224

Middleburg, FL 32050

DavisRaynesPublishing.com

Cover by Glowing Moon Designs

Formatting by Glowing Moon Designs

DavisRaynesPublishing.com

Witching After Forty follows the misadventures of Ava Harper – a forty-something necromancer with a light witchy side that you wouldn't expect from someone who can raise the dead. Join Ava as she learns how to start over after losing the love of her life, in this new paranormal women's fiction series with a touch of cozy mystery, magic, and a whole lot of mayhem.

A Ghoulish Midlife
Cookies for Satan (Christmas novella)
I'm With Cupid (Valentine novella)
A Cursed Midlife
Feeding Them Won't Make Them Grow (Novella in the Charity Anthology, Eat Your Heart Out)
A Girlfriend For Mr. Snoozerton (Novella)
A Haunting Midlife
An Animated Midlife
A Killer Midlife
More coming soon

CHAPTER ONE

"Coming!" I called.

The persistent knocking on the door roused me from a dead sleep. I'd just settled into the deep bliss of dreamland. And my crazy house didn't help. Every time whoever-was-about-to-get-an-earful-from-me-for-waking-me knocked on the door, the house echoed the sound upstairs, and I would've sworn it was doing it on purpose. Right outside my bedroom door. The last double tap was so loud I jumped out of bed. Literally landing on my buttocks on the hardwood floor, and then I understood why they were called *hard*wood.

Rubbing my behind, I stomped down the stairs, paying back the house for waking me. Whoever it was could have left a message and went away. I'd call them back, maybe. Eventually.

The last time someone woke me up this persistently, a skeleton stood on the other side of the door.

"Where is everyone?" I mumbled loudly. I'd told Alfred not to answer the door unless he knew who it was, but my son was here for the weekend, and Owen, my friend, roommate, and teacher, was hanging around somewhere. Apparently, neither of them was home.

As long as our new houseguest, the fully defleshed skeleton, Larry, didn't answer, we'd be okay. It was way too fudging early to deal with the aftermath of anyone seeing him.

Alfred stood beside the door, dry-washing his hands. He shrugged at me, his eyes somehow looking worried even though he couldn't move the skin on his face to convey that emotion. "It's okay," I said softly. "Just stand behind the door."

As my ghoul, Alfred had become a beloved member of our family, even if he wouldn't let me take out the strings tying his lips together. His vocal cords definitely worked, because he made grunting noises all the time. I've even caught him mumbling to Snooze once. So he *could* talk. I wasn't sure why he didn't *want* to. But I filed it under one of the many mysteries of life I didn't have time to solve at the moment. There was something about him he wanted to keep hidden. But hey, who was I to judge? I'd kept my necromancer side squashed for over twenty years.

Sometimes we suppressed part of who we were, and that was okay. So I wasn't about to push him to share his secrets.

Peeking out the peephole, I frowned. Nobody out there. "Probably some town kid playing a prank," I muttered. We had the spooky old house on the hill. Well, spooky with fresh paint and newly renovated insides.

I'd been thinking about doing some major upgrades, but at the last minute decided to restore the old house and keep the historical value of it. Although the value may have been zero since the house was basically alive. It wasn't possessed or anything, it was just... animated. My theory was the house had absorbed so much magic through the centuries that it formed its own spirit along the way.

I opened the door cautiously in case there really was someone out there. Couldn't be too careful after the winter we'd had. Murders and Satanic Christmas parties and all that. It had been chaos. The neighborhood was going to Hell.

Or was that just my new devilish neighbor? Definitely was Luci because I was going to send him there. Hopefully soon.

Casting thoughts of the devil aside, for now, I frowned at the absence of a warm body—or cold body, with my luck—standing on my porch. But instead of being greeted by a person, I stepped back when an envelope fluttered into the house and hung suspended in my entryway.

"Er, okay." The envelope turned toward me when I spoke and froze in midair, leaving the front so I could clearly read my name written in bold red calligraphy. Ava Calliope Howe Harper. Wow. They'd middle-named me. I hadn't been middle-named since I was a teenager living here with Yaya and Aunt Winnie.

What the heck was I supposed to do now?

I plucked the envelope from the air as Alfred shut the door behind us. He moved closer as if curious as to what it was. That made two of us.

"What've you got?" Owen walked down the stairs smoothing back his long black hair. He looked freshly showered, which explained why he hadn't answered the door.

I lifted one brow, at least I thought I did. Usually, I ended up moving them in all directions while

4

trying to lift only one. "Where were you? Did you not hear the door?" He was a morning person. I wasn't. This was his time to be adulty.

"I was in the shower." He studied me for a moment. "What's wrong with your eyebrows?"

"Nothing." I waved him off and focused on the envelope, then answered his question. "This floated into the house when I opened the door. I'm hoping it's not cursed." I laughed even though I was being serious.

We all walked into the large kitchen and sat at the table. I spied my son, Wallie, on the porch drinking coffee. We'd opened up the back wall of the kitchen to let in more light. Half of the back of the kitchen led into a large conservatory where we grew herbs and plants mostly for use in spells. The space was big enough, I could put in a small antique wood burning stove and a workstation for me to do my potions and spell casting. The ritual room in the attic was used for bigger magical things. Like accidentally conjuring Satan last Christmas.

Before we'd knocked down the wall, we had to go through the conservatory to reach the back deck, but thanks to a little elbow grease and a lot of magic, big French doors now also led to the porch from the kitchen.

I didn't blame Wallie for having his coffee out there. We'd recently learned how to create heat bubbles around ourselves, something among the *many* things Owen had taught us. Since I'd rejected my necromancer side and strongly suppressed even my elemental magic all my life, I'd had to relearn all the things my mother, aunt, and grandmother had taught me as a child and teen.

Plus, there was a whole world of magic I'd never given them the chance to share with me. One of my biggest regrets now that they were all gone.

"Alfred, will you get Wallie?" I said studying the envelope. A hum of magic flowed from it, telling me another witch had sent it.

Alfie grunted and tapped on the glass in the door, making Wallie jump and turn with wide eyes. Then he laughed when he realized he'd been startled by the house ghoul. I chuckled softly.

Larry and our big, fat Maine coon cat Snoozle walked in behind Alfred. Mr. Snoozleton, to be precise, but he was called all sorts of things.

"Good morning," Larry said. "I hope you're all well on this lovely winter morn."

Good grief, the skeleton was a morning undead person. I didn't do morning or morning people, undead or alive. Flesh or no flesh.

I had to force myself not to roll my eyes at the skeleton's turn of phrase. Or the fact that it still creeped me out that he could speak so eloquently without the aid of any *vocal cords*. Or a tongue, for that matter.

"The doorbell rang," I explained. "Then someone knocked until I answered, but nobody was there. Just this envelope."

Larry leaned close and his head pulled back as the sound of sniffing filled the air. "Smells like magic," he whispered.

How...? Nope. No, I wasn't going to ask how the skeleton could smell. Nope, not asking. *Just go with the crazy.*

"Hello?" A voice from the front door made me turn my head, but I didn't get up. I knew who it was before she spoke.

"Come in, Olivia!" I yelled. She came over all the time, but I didn't mind. She'd quickly become my best friend and partner in crime, even though we'd been enemies in high school.

Times changed us all. Life changed us. "Get in here," I called. "I got a mysterious letter."

She hurried into the kitchen with her arms full. Of course, she'd cooked. I looked up at her and spied a big pink box. Nope, she brought donuts this time.

Her son, Sammie, scurried in the room, arms held out toward Snoozle. Nice to see how I ranked with the kid. Did he not know I was the closest thing to an aunt he'd ever have?

Snooze hunkered down, but he let Sammie pick him up and hug him. "Hello Mr. Snoozer," Sammie said. "I missed you."

The look Snooze shot me made me snort. There was real panic in his eyes.

"Okay, he loves you, too," Olivia told Sammie. "Put him down."

Alfred grunted and Sammie launched himself into Alfie's arms. "Hey, Alf!" he cried. "I missed you, too."

Alfred grunted a few more times, which Sammie apparently understood because they ran out of the room and thundered up the stairs as Olivia's husband and my lifetime best friend, Sam, walked in.

"You shouldn't have given Alfred an iPad," Sam said. "Now Sammie wants one. He's been driving us nuts about it."

I blanched and shrugged while hiding my smile. "Sorry, friend. I had to have a way to communicate with Alfred. I don't speak grunts."

"What is that?" Olivia asked, setting the donuts on the table.

"A magical envelope." I smiled at her.

"Will you open that thing already?" Owen asked. "I'm dying to know what it is."

"As am I," Larry said pompously as he sat in one of the kitchen chairs. His pelvic bones clacked against the wood of the chair.

I closed my eyes briefly, hoping no parts fell off him.

Tearing my gaze away from the still-shocking sight of a skeleton at my kitchen table, I ripped the back of the envelope open.

The parchment inside was the thickest I've seen and probably expensive. I unfolded it and read the contents to the room.

Dear Ms. Howe-Harper,

The Shipton Harbor Coven cordially invites Ava Howe-Harper, Wallace Harper, and Owen Daniels to the monthly coven meeting this Saturday at 8 pm. It will be held at the home of the Coven Master. Repeat the spell on the bottom of this paper when you are ready to travel, and the direction will be made clear to you.

With Respect,
Bevan Magnus

Recruiter

Princeps invenire pythonissam

"Is that the spell?" Olivia whispered. Her eyes were wide and excited as she bent over my shoulder. "Can I go?"

"Yes. It means something along the lines of *Find the High Witch*. And no," I said evenly. "Because I'm not going. These people ostracized Aunt Winnie and Yaya because of my dad. No way."

I crumpled the parchment and tossed it on the table. As soon as it landed, it started opening up from its ball. Within seconds it was smooth as when I pulled it out of the envelope. I pointed and said, "See? Cursed."

Owen stared at it. "It's not cursed."

Yet he eyed it like it was going to attack him. *Ha, not so sure, are we?*

"I thought they invited your mom," Sam said. "But I don't remember the details."

I sighed and looked around the table at my new family. "They invited Mom, but Winnie and Yaya always said it was because they wanted an in with a powerful necromancer. Which never made sense to me since they once hated my dad for that same reason. Back then, I wasn't suppressing my power, and they sensed how strong I would be. When Mom died, Winnie withdrew from the coven, and I began to suppress my powers. Yaya and Winnie wouldn't force me to use them, so the coven sort of shunned them. Yaya stayed in because of, as she said it, keeping her enemies close, but she was basically trolling them."

They'd treated her like crap. We never got invitations to the witch parties, I was never invited to play with the other children of the coven, and once Winnie had pulled away and stopped being social after Mom died, her invitations dried up as well.

"I loved my coven in Nebraska," Owen said. "It was like a big family. Maybe this one has changed." He raised his eyebrows. "What would it hurt to go see?"

I tapped the parchment that wouldn't die. "Bevan Magnus was one of the ones that could've made us feel welcome after Mom died and could've tried to get us back in the fold. But no, he did nothing but stick his nose up at us. I'm telling you, they're not good people."

"I'd like to go, too," Wallie said. "I'd like to meet

LIA DAVIS & L.A. BORUFF

other witches. This Magnus might be a jerk, but they can't all be. And it's hard to meet our kind without the coven network." He grinned. "Michelle took me to meet her coven. It was awesome."

Michelle, his witch girlfriend, had come home with him for Christmas. Some big exam had kept her on campus this past weekend, but she was a sweet girl.

I sighed and stared at Owen and Wallie's hopeful expressions. "Fine," I growled. "We'll go. But mark my words. These witches are bitches."

CHAPTER TWO

With a sigh, I stood and grabbed a donut from the box. Then I pointed to Sam and Wallie. "What are you two doing here on a Tuesday morning, anyway?"

Sam grinned. "I'm off. I came to take Wallie and Sammie ice fishing."

Wallie grinned from ear to ear. "I've been dying to go."

"Aren't you due in class?" I asked.

He shook his head. "My classes on Mondays and Tuesdays are online, and I worked ahead. I'll drive back to campus in the morning."

I walked around the table and grabbed Sam's hair, yanking his head back to pop a rough kiss on his forehead. "Love you." He knew the kiss was thanks for taking Wallie along.

He beamed up at me. "Love you, too. I'm leaving Olivia with you for the day."

His wife and my newest friend snorted. "I'm a frikkin' delight," she said dryly.

Sam including Wallie in ice fishing with Sammie made me love my best friend all that much more. Sam and I grew up together. His parents owned the house just down the road, and he'd been the closest child to me. We'd never had the first inkling of a romantic feeling for one another. So much so that Olivia, while she'd been somewhat jealous at first of our unique sibling-like relationship, had soon seen that was all it was.

Sam was my brother from another mother... and father.

I refilled my coffee cup and bit into the donut with a moan. "Well, I'm going to the grocery store, then when you master fishermen get back, Livvie and I will have a nice warm stew ready for all three of you. Sound good?"

I looked back at the table to see everyone nodding eagerly, even Larry the skeleton. "Larry, you don't eat," I reminded him.

"I can pretend," he said, staring at me with sightless eye sockets. "Pretending is almost as good."

Alrighty then. Not for the first time, I found myself wishing I'd raised him when he was... more a person and less a skeleton, like Alfred.

But I was pretty sure the circumstances around Alfie's death had somewhat mummified him, rather than leading to his decomposition. He looked like he fell straight out of a movie about ancient Egypt, without the white wrappings.

Then again, I didn't know anything about Alfred's death or his raising since the necromancer who animated him was dead. Only Alfred knew and he wasn't talking. Literally.

Larry had been buried out in the woods, straight in the dirt. He'd decomposed quickly and easily. We still had to get his whole story, but I'd been waiting until Drew or Sam could be around to get the full statement. They'd have to be creative in their reporting, but they could still officially investigate the death.

"Larry, we'll go over your death tonight over dinner, okay?" I asked. "Sam will be here."

The skeleton nodded once. "Thank you."

He'd turned up Sunday, on Valentine's Day, just before my first date with the only man I'd been attracted to in the five years since my husband, and Wallie's father, died.

No way I was able to deal with a walking, talking skeleton then, so I'd allowed him to stay with us until we could figure out how to help him. Hey, what was one more undead under the roof? I was starting a collection.

Tonight, we'd get his full story and see what we could do to get him back in the ground and at peace.

"Well, we better get going," Sam said.

Wallie jumped up and nodded eagerly. "Back later, Mom. We'll have fresh fish for dinner!"

My heart swelled at the excitement in Wallie. Both of us had been just moving through the motions of everyday life. Who knew moving back to my hometown and releasing my powers would help us live again? Although, there was the murder of a family friend, William Combs, whom I inherited Alfred from, then I accidentally summoned Lucifer a few days before Christmas, who pretended to be Santa at the party and moved in next door. Life had been one crazy right after another.

Waving at the guys, I didn't say anything about the stew. I'd have it ready in case they didn't catch anything. And if they did, well, they'd be cleaning it, and I'd fry it up. I'd cook it, but no way I was pulling out all the guts and stuff. No, thanks.

I shuddered at the thought.

"Come on, Olivia," I said, wiping the donut film off my hands with the kitchen towel. "Let's hit the store."

She poured our coffees into two of my travel mugs, then handed me one. "Gimme your keys." She grinned. "I'll drive while you tell me about your date."

I pulled on my jacket and gave her a confused look. "I already told you."

"Yes," she said with a gleam in her eyes. "But I want to hear it again."

"I'll stay here," Owen called. "Don't worry about me."

We waved as we walked out the front door. "Okay!"

Once we pulled out of the driveaway, I tried to think of a way to tell the story differently. "I should have known the date was going to be derailed when we almost hit a ferret and the little shit flipped us the bird."

Olivia burst out laughing. "Are you serious?"

"As much as I am about sending Luci back to Hell."

She nodded, knowing that was serious business. "How could a ferret flip you the bird?"

"My guess is it was a shifter. But he looked rough and wild. I don't know anything about shifters or any other paranormal beings except witches and necromancers. And I even avoided them for most of my life." I looked out the window, knowing that was a mistake. Now that I was open to learning and controlling the growing magic inside me, I wished I had done it years ago.

Clay hadn't cared that I was a necromancer. It was his family who had looked down at me, and they didn't even realize I was more than a little *off* as his mother said once upon a time.

So, to keep the peace, I always kept my powers suppressed. I loved my husband and would've done anything to keep him happy. He'd felt the same way and had done everything in his power to make me and Wallie happy.

Shaking out of thoughts of my deceased husband, I went back to my recap of the big Valentine's Date with Sheriff Drew. "The restaurant was great; the food was great. We were alone in a public place, perfect for a first date. Then Luci showed with Carrie."

Olivia giggled. "Then everything got derailed."

"Yep. With a snap of Luci's fingers, we were in Paris, Tennessee. Then he snapped again, and we were in France." I laughed telling her how Lucifer twisted the history of the museum pieces at the Louvre and Carrie had corrected him each time.

We parked in the little grocery store's parking lot, and Olivia swooned. "That's amazing. Next time Lucifer decides to take you to France, stop in and get us! I could've dropped Sammie at Sam's parents' house."

I snorted. "It went so fast I didn't even think. I just tried to stay ahead of the whirlwind."

She sighed as we pulled out a buggy. "I can't believe sweet little Carrie."

"I know." I giggled. "She's got a hidden wildcat, I swear."

"She's not the only one."

Olivia and I jumped and whirled to find Sheriff Andrew Walker standing behind us in uniform. I let my eyes roam over him, drinking in his broad shoulders, thick muscled arms, and trim waist. His uniform fit him a little snug and left nothing to the imagination. In short, the man was hot. Also, he was the object of our conversation and had been my date on Valentine's Day.

In times like this moment, I forgot why I wanted

to take things slow with him. Then I started over-thinking and came back to reality. I still didn't know much about the sheriff.

"Hey, Drew," I whispered, meeting his teal eyes.

His dimple deepened as his smile did. "Hey, Ava."

A shudder went through me at the sound of his husky tone, and my insides melted.

"Well," Olivia said loudly. "I'm going to go pick out a big roast. We'd love to have you join us at Ava's for dinner, Drew," she said pointedly with a big smile plastered on her face.

"Be a little more obvious," I hissed, then turned back to Drew. "Yes, we would."

He ducked his head but waited until Olivia scurried away with the shopping cart before he replied. "I'd love to come for dinner," Drew said in a low voice. "But only if you're sure it'll be at your house. Our date Saturday was literally magical, and I had a wonderful time. And don't get me wrong, I don't regret going, but..." He looked around surreptitiously. "I threw up all day Sunday."

Gaping at him, I put my hand on his arm. "Oh, no. Are you okay?"

He nodded. "Yeah, I think so. It felt just like when I get motion sickness on a boat.

I poked out my bottom lip at the news he was sick, while inside I smiled a little. He'd shared something that most men wouldn't admit to. Now I knew he got motion sickness. That little peek into the mysterious Sheriff Drew made me want to know more.

"I did wonder why I hadn't heard from you," I murmured. "I'm sorry it was for such a bad reason."

He shrugged. "It was worth it. But maybe next time we just say no."

I snorted. "I'm not sure I know how to say no to Luci. But I'm going to be putting some effort in figuring out how to send him home, that's for sure."

Luci had been the unfortunate mishap of trying to summon Santa for a Christmas party. Instead of Santa, I'd gotten Satan.

Whoops.

But now I had to figure out how to send him back because he kept causing all kinds of chaos and had *no* desire to go back to his Kingdom.

"Would you like to go out again?" Drew asked. "Hopefully just the two of us this time."

I'd had a really good time with him, after all. "Sure," I said softly. "Dinner and bowling?" I asked, to take the stress off of him having to plan.

He grinned. "It's a plan. But I have to warn you. I'm going to kick your ass at bowling."

I snorted. "You only think so, Walker. I'm the bowling champion of Philadelphia, Pennsylvania."

We'd made it around the produce section by now and were fairly close to the meat department.

He turned and took my hand, then looked deep into my eyes. "If you use magic to win, I'll lock you up."

I laughed so loud Olivia jumped and whirled around, knocking against the big meat case she'd been peering into. Ignoring my new best friend, I fingered a button on Drew's shirt and batted my lashes at him. "Darling, I don't need magic to out bowl you."

He took my hand and moved closer until our bodies almost touched. My blood boiled and my legs began to shake. Not to mention my girly parts were chanting a victory song. He kissed my palm and flashed me a dimple-filled smile. "We'll see."

Then he left.

Damn, that man was hot.

"Oh geez, you have it bad." Olivia sneaked up behind me and sighed.

I waved her off as I moved back to the produce to

get potatoes and carrots for the stew. "I have no idea what you're talking about."

I didn't have it bad. I had urges and some of them were a little wicked leaning on the naughty side. *Okay, so maybe I did have it bad.*

CHAPTER THREE

Olivia had the carrots chopped, and I'd just thrown the meat cubes into the big stockpot when the front door opened.

"Hello?" Wallie called from the foyer. "We come bearing fishes!"

When he walked in the kitchen, followed by Sammie and Sam, he held up a string of the saddest, smallest fish I'd ever seen.

I arched an eyebrow and looked at Sam, who shrugged. "It wasn't a biting day."

With a snort, I pointed to the back porch. "Owen, will you show Wallie how to clean them with magic?" He nodded and rose from the table where he'd been reading an ancient-looking book.

I waved my hand and focused on the water

Wallie had let drip from the little fishtails and it disappeared without a sound. Moving to the hall that led out to the front door, I did the same there.

Sam crossed to the sink and washed his hands while Sammie followed Wallie to the back porch.

Thirty minutes later, we had fish frying merrily in the skillet while the stew bubbled and cooked. It would take a while for the beef to be done, so the fish would make a nice appetizer while we waited. They weren't big enough for much else.

But my boy was proud of those little fish, and I was happy that he had a great time.

"Excuse me," Larry said as he wandered into the room. "Would now be a good time to talk about my murder?"

I sighed and sat at the table. "Yes, but the sheriff is on his way to eat with us. Let's wait until he gets here." No sense in going through it all twice.

The doorbell rang just seconds later. Alfred grunted and shuffled out of the room, followed closely by Sammie and Snooze.

My stomach clenched with nerves, even though I'd just seen Drew a few hours before at the store. "Do I look okay?" I whispered as I flipped the fish.

Olivia fluffed my hair. "You look great," she said, then raised her voice. "Hey, Drew. Come on in."

She acted like my house was hers, but that was how she was. A natural-born hostess. I didn't mind. Olivia and I were growing closer the more time we spent together.

"Great," Larry said. "Thanks for coming."

Drew jumped a little and his hand flew to his side where his gun was probably hiding under his jacket. "Oh, hey, Larry," he said. He'd met the skeleton after our date Sunday night.

And had shot him.

Larry gave Drew a dark look. "Hey," he muttered.

How had I known Larry had given Drew a dark look? Larry didn't have any skin! It was like a feeling I had that was most likely tied to my necromancer powers.

I was going to have to stop questioning this stuff. It just was what it was.

"So, everyone here? Can we do this?" Larry was starting to get a little testy.

"Yes," I said. I could listen just fine as I cooked. "Go ahead."

But Alfred shuffled over and took the spatula from my hands and grunted, giving me a little push toward the table.

"Thanks, Alfie," I said. I didn't like automatically

expecting him to cook or clean for me, but that seemed to be what he preferred to do.

I joined my friends at the table as Wallie came back downstairs. He'd gone up to shower and change after cleaning the fish. "Sammie is playing with Snooze and Alfred's iPad."

"Tell us what happened," I told Larry. "As best you remember it."

"Well, it was in the eighties. Eighty-nine." Larry clacked his fingers on the table.

The year after my mother died, I realized. She'd died in eighty-eight. Sam, who remembered it vividly, glanced at me out of the corner of his eye. I nodded once to acknowledge that we were both thinking the same thing.

"And were you a human or a witch?" Drew asked. He'd pulled out a little notebook.

"Witch," Larry replied. "Elemental. Air."

Drew's pencil scratched on the paper. "And how did you die?"

"I was sucked into a patch of quicksand," Larry said matter of factly.

"Where?" I asked. Maybe he'd been killed elsewhere and moved here.

"About a mile away, I'm guessing. It was hard to

tell how far I walked to get here." He shrugged one bony shoulder. "I can show you."

"Um, Larry?" Sam said. "There's no quicksand in Maine."

He nodded. "Exactly. I believe I was murdered by a witch."

"If you really sank in quicksand, it would've had to have been magical," Olivia said. "You can't actually *sink* in quicksand. The density isn't right. You'd go to your waist, maybe."

The skeleton spread his hands, palm up, as if to say, *see?*

"What was going on in your life at that time?" Drew asked.

"Well, I'd just joined the local coven. The same one you're going to go to a meeting with." He nodded toward me.

Drew looked at me with one eyebrow up, but I just shrugged. "Hey, I didn't want to go."

"Everything seemed perfect. But then I was walking in the woods, in the summer. I can't remember the month now. But I stumbled across someone deep in the trees. He was slitting the throat of a deer. It freaked me out because I felt the magic in the air and the sense of perversion. He was doing some intensely dark blood magic. I took off running, and the next thing I knew, I sank."

"What's the other side like?" Sam looked awestruck and his voice came out a whisper.

Larry sighed. "I don't remember. The last thing I remember is sinking. And then waking up and being pulled to Ava. Owen told me how long it's been."

Owen nodded. "Yes, Larry told me his story on Valentine's night while you two were off in Paris."

I couldn't stop the flush rising up my cheeks. "Is there anything else you remember about your death?" I asked, drawing the conversation back around to the skeleton and not my date.

"He slipped a coin in my pocket," he said. "At least, I think it was a coin. I was running, and he almost caught me. I kept running, but he stuffed something in my pocket. I figured I'd see what it was later, and it didn't occur to me it was causing me to sink. But in retrospect, I think it could've been a cursed coin. I remember a flash of silver."

"For it to be a cursed coin, it would've had to have been silver. Modern coins don't have enough precious metals in them to contain a curse. Nickel, zinc, copper, those metals won't hold a curse. It takes gold, platinum, but the most common is silver," Owen said.

I nodded in agreement. I'd known that; some leftover knowledge from my witch studies as a child.

"There are a number of coins made up until 1964 that are ninety percent silver," Olivia said.

"How do you know this random stuff?" Owen asked.

Sam patted Olivia's hand. "This woman is a trivia queen. Always try to be on her team in a trivia contest."

She blushed and nudged him with her shoulder.

I sighed and sat back in my chair. "Did you see the witch?" I asked.

Larry shook his head. "No, he wore a hood."

"So, it could've been a woman?" Sam asked.

"I suppose." Larry looked off in the distance as if thinking. "But the presence felt masculine. I don't know how to describe it." He blinked rapidly.

Wait. He couldn't have blinked! He didn't have eyes! Ugh, damn necromancer powers were making me crazy. Or I was just going insane.

"Your cat is chasing an animal in the backyard," Larry said and pointed out the door.

Alfred grunted and walked toward the door. At some point, he'd put on an apron that said *Kiss the Cook*. That silly ghoul.

A brief memory from my childhood flashed in

my mind. It was of my dad cooking with a similar apron. Frowning, I shook off the memory as Alfred grunted again and opened the back door, scurrying out with a big wooden spoon in his hand.

Leaving the back door standing open, he hurried out into the yard. I scraped my chair back and followed quickly to see what in the world Snooze had gotten into. There was no telling with that crazy fat cat.

I stood on the patio, surrounded by Drew, Sam, Wallie, and Olivia. Larry and Owen stepped down the porch steps.

"Is that a ferret?" Olivia asked.

Alfred stood by and waited for the mystery animal and Snooze to streak by, then at just the right moment he reached out and thwacked Snooze on the rump with his wooden spoon.

Snoozle stopped short and turned around toward Alfred with a yowl that sounded suspiciously like he was saying, "Ow!"

Alfred put both hands on his hips, glaring at the cat. Then he pointed to the back door with a stiff arm.

"What kind of relationship do these two have?" Olivia whispered.

Snooze hunched down and stalked toward the

house. He stopped at the stairs and turned to growl at Alfred.

Alfred stopped walking and put his hands on his hips again. He grunted once, and Snoozle walked past us and into the house.

Alfred waited for us to all follow Snooze back into the kitchen.

With a loud click, Alfred closed the front door and locked it. He nodded once at the lot of us, still close to the door with our heads turned toward the cat, staring at the spectacle, then went back to the stove to finish dinner.

"Ohm-kay. Anybody hungry?" I asked.

CHAPTER FOUR

*S*am's work phone squawked halfway through dinner. I internally groaned at the interruption. If Sam left, there was a good chance Drew would too.

Before we started eating, Alfred had urged Larry to go upstairs with him to do who knew what dead things did. I shuddered to think.

Honestly, they were probably just playing with furious birds on the tablet.

I bit into the fish, which was surprisingly tender and flaky, as Sam answered. "This is Thompson."

I couldn't hear whatever came over the line, but Sam's face darkened. That wasn't good. "Yeah, the sheriff is here with me."

Sam covered the mouthpiece. "We gotta go."

Drew's forehead creased and he pursed his lips.

"Okay, text me the address." He paused. "Oh, I know where that is." Another long pause. "Seriously? Okay, we're on our way."

"What is it?" Drew asked, scooting out his chair. "Why didn't they call me?"

Sam jumped up and shoveled several more bites in his mouth. "Said they did. Old Miss Miriam was killed at her shop," he mumbled around a potato.

Drew pulled out his phone. "Shit. It's on silent."

Larry and Alfred peeked down from the top of the stairs as we followed Sam and Drew to the door. "Sam, your uniform," Olivia said. Drew was still in his.

He shrugged. "It's okay. I can work a case in plain clothes. It's better that we get there fast."

As she pressed a kiss to Sam's cheek, I considered doing the same to Drew, but that felt *way* too intimate after we'd only had one date... And whatever dinner tonight could be considered. Not a date.

Even though we've kissed before, a couple of times, I didn't think we were at the point of the quick goodbye kisses.

"Should..." I looked around at my friends. "Maybe we should come."

Sam furrowed his brow. "Wasn't old Miss Miriam a friend of your Yaya's?"

I nodded. "Yeah. Which means she might be a witch."

Drew shook his head. "I don't think it's a good idea."

He and Sam exchanged a long look. "Maybe once we've assessed the situation, we'll have you come to the morgue, look for one of those witch's marks," Sam said.

I nodded. "Okay. Call us if you need us."

Drew glanced back, looking like he was considering the same kiss I had. He dipped his head and touched my hand briefly. "Good night."

Okay. Definitely too soon for the *have a good day at work, sweetie* kiss.

I watched them, Drew specifically, rush to Drew's patrol car as I slowly closed the door. Olivia tugged at my arm. When I glanced at her she giggled, which made me roll my eyes. I did not have it bad for the sheriff.

I had something, but it wasn't bad.

As a group, we shuffled back to the kitchen, with Alfred and Morty joining us. "Remind them to look for a coin," Larry said.

"Oh, good idea." Olivia pulled out her phone and sent a text to Sam.

When we entered the kitchen, I gasped and threw up my hands, ready to shoot a beam of... Hell, I didn't even know what I would've shot. It was instinct and my magic was ready to blast the intruder on my command.

Well, that was new. Maybe opening my senses to my power made it easier to access. Of course, it did. That meant I had to be careful and not be so impulsive. I didn't want to blow up my house or anyone.

I stared as Luci stood at the stove, dishing himself up a bowl of stew as Sammie kicked his legs at the table, eating and wearing most of his dinner. "This smells amazing," Luci said. "Sammie here tells me he caught this delectable fish. Good man, Sammie-boy."

Olivia rushed to sit beside her son. Her face was as white as, well, a ghost, which was one damn dead thing I'd yet to deal with—and had no desire to.

It was one thing for me to go on a date and end up double dating with Luci and Carrie. It was another thing to walk into the kitchen and find little Sammie happily eating with the devil himself.

"What are you doing here?" I scowled at him, crossing my arms.

He turned and winked at me. "I hear you've got a

corpse problem." Pausing with the ladle in one hand, he gaped at Larry. "Larry Parks? I wondered where you'd got off to."

Larry froze. "You know me?"

Luci nodded. "Of course! There are not many souls that escape Hell."

We all slowly turned to stare at Luci. "Larry was in Hell?"

"I mean, he was a witch. What do you think happens?" Luci shrugged and looked at all of us. "But don't worry. It's not all as bad as it's cracked up to be. I mean, sure, we torture evil souls for eternity, that much is right. But not everyone that comes to my domain is evil."

He walked to the table with his bowl of stew. "Even Hell needs bureaucrats."

"How'd you recognize me?" Larry asked.

"I never forget a face," Luci said. I wasn't touching that comment. "How are you? What are you doing here?"

Never forget a face. I studied the skeleton for a long moment, trying to find the face Lucifer mentioned. Nope, just a skull.

Larry glanced at me. Like turned his eyeless, fleshless face toward me. Then he directed his attention back to Luci. "Man, do you know who murdered me?"

Luci sighed and sat down while the rest of us stood in a huddle and gaped at him. All but Olivia, who had her arm around Sammie, glaring. "I'm sorry, Larry, I don't. I'm not privy to most things that happen up here. Unless Larry knew and told me himself, I wouldn't have that 411. Or maybe when his murderer dies, I'll find out then. But in the meantime? Zip. That's why this time here with you all is so fun." He grinned and took a big bite. "Oh, heaven. Absolute heaven. Nothing like a good winter stew." He seemed to realize for the first time we weren't all comfortable with him there. "What?" he asked. "Sit. Eat."

I would figure out a way to get this—erm, man?— back to Hell. In the meantime, I surely didn't want to piss him off.

"Thank you," I said. "Alfred and I made it."

Luci narrowed his eyes at Alfred, and to my shock, Alfred was glaring right back. "I'm afraid I don't know your Alfred. Either he looked different from his persona in my realm, or he'd been in Heaven before he was resurrected." Luci shrugged. "Either way, I get the feeling he's not a big fan."

"Alfred is just ornery," I said. "That's all. He means no offense, do you, Alfie?"

Shaking his head and looking away, Alfred shuffled over to the stove and began rinsing out dishes, preparing them for the dishwasher.

"What was all the kerfuffle about?" Luci asked. "Where'd the handsome Sheriff and Deputy go?"

"There was a death in town," I said as I tried to relax and act normal. I didn't think he meant us any harm, but he was volatile and unpredictable at best.

"Oh?" Luci's eyes flashed and he leaned forward conspiratorially. "I thought I heard something about you wanting to go. Is that true?"

Nosey much? I nodded. "We'd like to know if this murder relates to Larry's." Or my mother's, but we had no proof that her death was the fault of anything but a freak lightning storm. But two murders so close to each other over thirty years ago raised a butt load of suspicion inside me. Especially when the two who died were witches.

Then it dawned on me that Larry might have known Aunt Winnie.

Luci tapped his nose. "I've just the thing. Come here."

Larry, Alfred, and Sammie jumped up as the rest

of us did, but Luci winked at them. "Alfie, be a good man and take the children out to play, would you?"

Snoozle growled from the corner. I hadn't even realized he was in the room. "Shoo," I said.

"Cute cat," Luci drolled. "Okay, now if I can draw everyone's attention to the pot of soup."

"Stew," I muttered, then glanced up to see Luci arching an eyebrow at me. "Sorry," I whispered.

He winked at me again and waved his hand over the pot. I leaned in closer and Olivia did the same on the other side of Luci. We watched as the dark liquid began to swirl as if it was being stirred by an invisible spoon.

The stew stirred faster until an image formed in the center of the whirlpool in the pot. I'd seen Yaya and Winnie do this type of scrying before. I've even attempted it a few times but never mastered it. Maybe since I was all open to my full powers, I could.

Focusing on the image in the stew, I scrunched up my nose and tilted my head to the side. "Is she wrapped in yarn?"

Luci nodded. "It appears her auto-knitting machine went on the fritz and trapped her in a skein of yarn."

"That's crazy," I said in disbelief.

"A freak accident," Olivia added.

Larry leaned over my shoulder, resting his skull on it. I tried not to jerk away from him. I didn't want his head falling into the stew pot. "Magical accident."

Luci eyed the scene with a raised brow. "I'd have to agree with Larry. But what a way to go. Death by a yarn cocoon."

"Lucifer! That's not funny." I pushed him, but the demon didn't move. He just laughed.

Poor Miss. Miriam.

Just then Drew and Sam came into view. Drew directed another officer to cut her out of the yarn.

We watched in fascination as she was cut out. Sam put on latex gloves, knelt, and searched her pockets. After reaching in the second pocket of her long coat, he pulled out a coin.

The coin was nothing like I'd seen before. It was silver and looked to be as big as silver dollar. Then again it was hard to tell from a vision in a pot of stew. It had a bird that was surrounded by flames.

"That's it!" Larry jumped with excitement. "That's the coin the witch put in my pocket."

CHAPTER FIVE

"*N*ot like that!" Owen called. "You've got to *mean* it. If anything is buried nearby, you'll raise it."

I sighed and sat back down. We'd been at it for hours, practicing while everyone else was busy with their lives. Wallie was back at college, Olivia was doing her turn as room mother for Sammie's kindergarten class, and Sam and Drew were working the murder case. Not that there'd been any leads. A big crock of nothing. I would've much rather worked the murder case with them, but I did need to learn to work my powers more effectively.

Snooze was on his back all stretched out in a patch of sunlight. Snoozing, of all things. Did I tell you that's how he got his name? That lazy cat was a master of naptime.

Larry and Alfred had opted to stay back at the house. Wallie had left some game system for them, something he said he never played anymore, and they were hooked. They'd been in my living room all week learning how to use the controls.

Owen's words brought me back to what I was supposed to be paying attention to. "Focus on just this clearing. I sense several small critters that have died and been interred to the ground within the clearing. You should be able to find them and raise them, even if it's for a brief time."

"I'll end up with another skeleton in my guest room," I grumbled. At this rate, I was going to run out of rooms soon. But then I sucked in a deep breath and tried again. I'd never get better at this or be able to use it for good if I didn't practice. I was supposed to be super powerful, but I couldn't even sense all the bodies that Owen could.

Closing my eyes, I cleared out all my thoughts and imagined I was in a pitch-black room of nothingness. Thoughts of Drew tried to enter my dark space, but I pushed him out. Not the time to think about the sexy sheriff. I had dead things to find.

Once I chased Sheriff Hottie out of my head, I

got down to business. A calm washed over me as I stretched out my senses. The ground under me warmed and energy drifted up and circled me. The low pulse of earth magic reached out to me. I opened to it, and let it direct me to what I was searching for.

The half of me that was witch was elemental. But all witches used nature and the earth to draw power from. I used that natural energy to search for the dead animals buried in a small clearing.

Finally, I felt one. A few feet to my left, something small rested there, and recently dead. I turned to find it, but the ground looked undisturbed. Odd. A body that fresh should've had some sort of sign. The freshly dug dirt or something. An animal dying of natural causes in the woods should've been just lying on the ground, come to think of it. Not buried.

Focusing on the small animal, I breathed deep and pushed my magic into it.

Without warning, Snooze sat up and yowled at me, making me start and breaking my concentration. At almost the same time, dirt exploded from the ground and an animal streaked across the clearing, straight for me.

I screeched and held up my hands, reacting without thinking, blasting the little guy with whatever magic chose to come out of me.

The animal flew to the side and Snooze pounced, growling, tail swinging wildly.

Seconds later, the small animal, which I was pretty sure was another ferret—what the heck was going on with ferrets lately?—morphed into a naked, dead young man.

Mr. Snoozerton, the big, strong kitty cat, who had been so vicious moments before with the little ferret, squealed like a stuck pig and streaked off in the direction of the house, yowling at the top of his voice.

"Coward," I whispered.

"What the shit?" Owen gasped. We both scrambled to our feet as the boy rolled over.

Owen yanked off his jacket and threw it over the teen to give him some modesty. "Who are you?" I asked.

He opened his eyes, and they were filmy and cloudy. "Who's there?" he whispered.

"My name is Ava," I said. "I was trying to raise an animal, but I didn't know you were a shifter."

The teen struggled to sit up. Owen put his arm around the boy, and I grabbed his hand. "What happened to you, son?"

When I got close, the smell hit me. Necromancy was not a glamorous branch of witchcraft. Not by a longshot. This poor kid smelled like he'd been dead a while. Looked it, too. His skin was mottled and rotting away in some places. "What happened?" I asked.

"I was killed in a shifter fighting ring," he whispered. "But I don't know where it was. I was forced to shift with magic and put in a dark box until it was time to fight. I think I was used as bait." He looked around, but I had no idea how much he could see with his milky eyes.

Then again, Larry saw fine with *no* eyes, so who knew?

My stomach twisted while anger made my blood run hot as I processed the boy's words. A shifter fighting ring? Of all the horrible news! "Sweetie, did you recognize anyone? Or hear any names?"

The boy closed his eyes and let his head relax against Owen's chest. "No," he whispered. "They were really careful, and I wasn't there all that long."

He continued trying to look around. "Can you take me back to my parents?"

"Of course, sweetie." I put my hand on his arm. "What's your name and your parents' names?"

He blinked rapidly. "I'm Ricky Johnson, and my mom is Dana, and my daddy is also Ricky."

Owen gave me a significant look. "Let him go," he said. "Release the magic animating him."

Focusing on the boy's mottled forehead, I imagined cutting the magic source from him.

It worked. He slumped in Owen's arms, then as quickly as he'd shifted into a person, he shifted back to a ferret. "Why did he shift back?" I asked.

"Shifters die in whatever form they're in. His body is at peace as a ferret, and his soul is at peace. I don't know if you could feel it, but he didn't want to be here."

I nodded rapidly. "I did feel that!" There had been a resistance I never got from the ghoul or skeleton currently in my home. Or Snoozer. "Is that why Larry and Alfred are so difficult to let go?"

Owen nodded as he wrapped the little furry body in his jacket. "They cling to life. Those at peace fight it."

That made sense, at least. And it meant I'd know if ever I tried to bring someone back, if they had found paradise. That might be why I hadn't been able to heal or bring back my mom when she died.

I gathered the little guy up in Owen's jacket. "Let's get him to his parents."

A SIMPLE INTERNET search gave us the info we needed. Rick and Dana lived two towns over, about a forty-five-minute drive. I grabbed a small box and wrapped little Ricky up in my prettiest kitchen towel, then filled Alfie and Larry in on where we were headed. This boy's parents deserved to have their son back.

We pulled up to the address an hour later, after stopping along the way for a pee break. Neither Owen nor I were any sort of spring chicken, and a bathroom pit stop had been required.

Sucking in a deep breath, I climbed the steps of the small, rundown bungalow, and rapped on the screen door with my knuckles.

A small woman with wide hips and curly dark hair answered. "Yes?" she asked guardedly. "Can I help you?"

"Ma'am, my name is Ava, and this is my friend, Owen. Are you Dana Johnson?" My heart ached for this poor woman and what I was going to have to tell her shortly.

She nodded with a stricken look on her face. She knew what I was going to be telling her. A mother always knows.

"Is your husband home?" I asked.

She nodded. "Yes. What's this about?"

"I'm sorry, ma'am, but we have news about your son, Ricky." I pursed my lips. "Can we come in?"

Tears filled Ms. Johnson's eyes as she unlocked the screen door. "Yes, come in."

"Rick!" she yelled. "Get in here!"

Rick walked in, tall and lanky, reminiscent of the boy who had died in Owen's arms. Re-died. Ugh.

Damn. I didn't want to do this. I should have called Sam to do it while I hung out with the scaredy-cat, Snooze. Sam was a cop, surely he had experience with telling loved ones bad news.

"Please, sit," Ms. Johnson said. "I'm sorry, your names again?"

"Mr. Johnson," I nodded at the man as he put his arm around his wife and introduced Owen and myself again. "We're here about your son."

I leaned forward and put the shoebox on the coffee table. A sob caught in Ms. Johnson's throat. "What is that?"

"Ma'am, I'm a necromancer," I whispered. I cringed because I hadn't said that out loud to strangers before. "I was out in the woods near to my home in Shipton Harbor this morning, practicing my craft. I raised a small animal, and when he came above ground, he shifted into your son."

Dana sucked in a breath and covered her mouth

with her hands. Tears filled her eyes. Rick stared at the box for a long time before he finally picked it up. His hands shook as he took off the lid.

Sobs came from Dana and she reached inside to touch little Ricky. "He's so cold. Rick, he's cold."

Mr. Johnson curled an arm around his wife and held her to him. "I know baby. But he's home now."

The couple held each other with their son in a box in their lap. It was all I could do to keep my waterworks from breaking the dam holding them back.

When they'd calmed down, they clutched the box between them and glared at Owen and me. The father asked, "What did he say?"

"He said that he'd died as the result of being..." I sucked in my breath and searched myself for strength. "He was a bait animal in a shifter fighting ring."

This so sucked. I hated every part of it. My heart ached for the couple. But what else could I do? They had to know.

Dana cried harder while Rick worked his jaw. His anger was outweighing his sorrow. I wasn't sure if that was good or not. I would've been angry in his place, for sure. Hell, little Ricky wasn't my kid, and I was angry.

"If you want us to take this to the police," I said. "I can call in the sheriff of Shipton Harbor. He knows about the supernatural world."

They shook their heads quickly and vehemently. "No. We'll handle this among the pack. Shifters..." Rick squeezed his wife. "We're private. We don't generally like interference from humans."

Owen nodded. "I figured as much. That's why we didn't do it, to begin with."

"Is there anything we can do?" I was growing a little antsy, wanting to call Wallie and tell him I loved him. Plus, I didn't want to start crying in front of these poor people. "I can help with any funeral costs."

If I didn't have the money, Olivia and I could start a fundraiser for the family.

The couple stood. They shook their heads but didn't refuse or accept any funeral help. I'd check on them in a few days and offer again. Owen and I stood as well, then Dana rushed at me and hugged me. "Thank you for bringing my baby home."

"It was the least I could do. I have a son. I can't imagine..." I let the statement drift off. When Dana released me, I conjured my notepad and pen from the phone table in my hallway at home. After writing my name and number down, I tore off the page and handed it to Dana. "If there is anything you need, just call. I'm usually up late and sleep in, but Owen is an early bird."

"Thank you," Dana said, walking us to the door.

I handed the keys to Owen and climbed into the passenger seat. First, on the drive home, I called my son and thanked him for not being a shifter and for still being alive. He was confused but played along, promising he had no plans on dying.

After I hung up, I cried the rest of the way home.

CHAPTER SIX

*E*ven though we said we wouldn't, I ended up filling Drew in on what had happened with poor little Ricky. In my defense, the sheriff called me not long after Owen and I got home, and my emotions were still raw. By that time fury at what the boy must have gone through had mixed with my sorrow for his parents.

I tried to play it off as allergies and a scratchy throat, but, no, Drew was too intuitive to fall for my lies. He came over and I spilled everything. Even a few more tears. He knew how shifters were and promised to keep the information unofficial, even though I knew he'd be investigating the best he could off the records.

And so would I.

The shifters would be trying to track this fighting ring and deal with it their own way if they found them before we did.

I didn't really care who found Ricky's murderers, as long as they were found and punished.

But I had to put that in the back of my mind, because Owen, Wallie, and I were ready to go to the Coven meeting. I hadn't been able to talk them out of it. That meant I had to go. Double ugh.

Wallie had driven home as soon as he finished his afternoon class last night. I pulled the mom-card and told him he didn't need to be driving back and forth so much. It was a four-hour drive one way. A lot could happen.

He'd just stared at me with a raised brow, reminding me so much of his father.

So here we were, standing in my living room ready to go face the witches.

"Princeps invenire pythonissam."

We waited for the spell to reveal the who and where and nothing happened. "Well, we must have been uninvited." I started to walk off but Wallie grabbed my hand.

"We can try it in the car. Maybe it'll work when it knows you are making an effort."

I huffed. "I *am* making an effort." To not go. Didn't say that last part though...

Owen and Wallie didn't buy it. They stared until I gave in.

"Okay." I rolled my eyes and stomped out of the door and to my car. You know, for effect.

Once in the car and the engine started, I repeated the spell. Owen drove, I navigated. "Let's do this."

And my too-smart-for-his-own-good son was right. Darn it. The spell worked.

"Mom," Wallie said as we drove down a long stretch of road by the coast. "What are we doing about our house in Philly?"

I sighed and turned in my seat to face my son. "That is a conversation we need to have. It's the home you grew up in, yet it isn't *my* home. Not really, and not anymore." As hard as it would be to say goodbye to the house I'd lived in with my Clay, I knew my place was in Shipton Harbor. I wasn't meant to live in Pennsylvania anymore. "Do you want to move back there after college?" I asked.

Wallie shook his head. "No. I know I should since it's technically my hometown. But I want to come to Shipton. I feel like I belong here as much as you do."

I smiled and reached back to pat his leg. "Then we'll sell the house. We should get a nice bit of profit for what we've already paid off on the loan. We'll put that aside and you can use it for starting out in life. I think your father would love knowing he helped you get your start with the home he worked hard to pay for."

Wallie nodded and squeezed my hand. "Thanks, Mom."

I hummed, thinking how nice it would be to have Wallie so close all the time. "We have plenty of land. You could build a house and not even be all that close to me." On one side, our property ended near Lucifer's brand-new house.

But on the other side and back to the ocean, we had about ten acres. Most of it was woods or wild, untouched by any development. It would make for a gorgeous, secluded spot for Wallie's home.

Suddenly, the spell telling me where to go shifted direction. "Turn!" I squawked.

Owen slammed on the brakes and stopped in the middle of the road. "Left or right?"

I looked back and forth. "Oh, sorry. Left." I probably should've specified that when I yelled.

"I think we're close." Leaning forward, I

squinted out of the windshield and tried to see past the illumination of the car's headlights.

As we turned a corner, an enormous house came into view, suddenly visible once the car cleared the trees. The mansion was at least three-stories of gothic perfection. It even had a few gargoyles perched on the roof. Dark grey stone covered the exterior with red shutters that accented the windows only added to the witchy look of the building.

On either side of the front of the home, two round, tower-like structures melted in with the rest of the structure. My Victorian would be so jealous if he saw this. So I wouldn't be telling him. Wait, he might already know. This mansion in front of me had been the meeting place for the coven for as long as my family had owned my house. Maybe it had taken on a bit of personality as well.

We pulled right up to the front door and a teenager in a suit ran down the stairs. "Let me park your car for you, sir," he said as he rounded the car to Owen.

Since it was my vehicle, Owen raised his eyebrows at me. I nodded once, so he handed the keys to the young man while Wallie and I got out and shut our car doors.

When we reached the front door of the mansion,

it opened without warning. We stepped inside to find nobody holding it. "Ohh," I whispered in a sing-song voice. "Magic."

A thrill went through me. It felt good to be around others that were open with their magic. Even though I still didn't trust most of the members of the coven or their intentions for wanting me—a necromancer—to be inducted into their inner circle.

Owen and Wallie chuckled as we moved farther into the entryway. The interior was a mix of contemporary and gothic style. A black cast iron spiral staircase sat to our left that was wide enough for two people to walk up, side by side. The floors were white and black marble. I wasn't sure if it was real marble or just ceramic flooring made to look like it. But with how elegant the house was, I was going with the former.

The white walls had dark grey trim, while the doors were all black, sticking with the gothic theme.

"This place is amazing." I'd have to seriously talk with Winston—my house—about some upgrades. That would mean he'd have to let strangers inside to make said changes. I couldn't do all of it with magic, and he was still mad at me for wanting to sell him.

Soft footsteps brought my attention to another

teenager, a girl this time, exiting a doorway to our right. "Please, allow me to take your coats."

She smiled eagerly, her blonde hair in a long braid down one side of her head. I had no trouble imagining her in a bouncy cheerleader uniform.

"Friends," a rich female voice drifted across the large entryway. "Thank you so much for coming." We turned to find a woman walking serenely out of a large double door to an impressive library.

"Cynthia," I said. "How nice to see you." Ugh. I hated putting on this face, this fakeness. But that's what it took to be in a coven. *This* coven, at least.

Cynthia was beautiful and youthful. Her blond hair was gathered in a neat bun at the base of her neck. A few curly strands hung loose to frame her pale, heart-shaped face. She had brown eyes that had flecks of silver through them. It was an odd mix of colors but worked on her.

"Please, call me CeCe. And come in. We were just about to get started." She stepped to the side and held out her arm for us to enter the library.

We walked in to find eight or nine witches sitting in a circle. Men and women I'd known off and on all my life, mostly. There were a few faces I didn't recognize.

"Please, sit," a man said. He stood and smiled,

but the distaste rolled off of him like a stinky cologne. I had to stop myself from curling my lip at him. For whatever reason, he didn't like me or maybe Owen. Maybe both, since we were necromancers. He'd have no reason to dislike Wallie. Nobody here knew him. I doubted these people even knew he was my son. Except the invitation had included his name. Maybe they did.

"We were just about to have a drink to the memory of our beloved lost coven member, Miriam Buckner." A tray floated toward us with three champagne flutes resting on it. I took one, pretending the act of magic was no big deal. Even though I'd begun doing much more with magic myself, now that I'd fully embraced my magical side, I still felt like a fish at a bird convention with all these lifelong practitioners around me.

The man, the one who didn't seem to like us, spoke first. "To Miriam. A blessed friend and sister to us all. She will be missed. May her next journey be all she wants it to be."

CeCe raised her glass and looked around the room. "Now, we will continue to honor our fallen sister in our actions and deeds." She sighed and looked at the man who had given the toast. "Bevan," she paused and looked at me. "Bevan Magnus, our recruiter, secretary, pretty much a jack of all trades, eh, Magnus?"

Magnus nodded his head once at her as more disapproval flowed off of him. Surely, I wasn't the only one who could feel it?

"Bevan will update us on the reunion at the Witch Academy," CeCe said, then gave Bevan her full attention.

Well, heck. I hadn't even attended the witch academy. Once I'd told Yaya and Aunt Winnie, I didn't want anything to do with it, they'd left me alone about witch stuff. Part of me wished now I hadn't done it, but it was what it was.

"The reunion planning is moving along smoothly. All invitations have been sent out. Catering selections were finalized." Bevan smiled at everyone in the room except for me.

Yeah, the feeling's mutual, buddy. Something about him didn't sit right with me.

CeCe took the floor with the last few items on an agenda that I hadn't seen. I guessed I had to be a member to see the meeting's to-do list. "And the final current business is the New Moon Ritual. This month it will be held at Bevan's house. Don't forget to sign up to bring a treat or drink."

Oh, the New Moon Ritual sounded nice. I bet Olivia would've loved to see it.

"It's a real shame that your mom and grandmother aren't with us to attend the reunion," a woman said as she walked up to us. "Hi, I'm Lorelai."

She smiled, and her apple cheeks and red lips dazzled under kind blue eyes and perfectly coiffed honey-blonde hair. She looked like she could step into any boardroom and take complete charge. At the same time, I had no trouble picturing her in jeans and a sweater, teaching kindergarteners.

"Ava. But I guess you know that." I laughed softly, completely out of my element. There were too many mixed energies here that made me a little uneasy.

Lorelai smiled at me and it felt genuine. I liked her. "I was friends with your Aunt Winnie at the Witch Academy," she said. "And our Bevan went through with your mother."

I raised my eyebrows. "Oh, really?" I hadn't realized he knew my mom.

Lorelai nodded. "Indeed. They invited your mother and Winnie to join the coven, but both declined at first. Of course, you know your mother was in the process of joining when she died." She sniffed and dabbed at her eyes. "A tragedy."

The older woman seemed sincere, but who could truly tell with these people? "That's when Bevan moved here," she continued. "I suppose word got around the Academy that your aunt was considering not joining us, and there was an opening. Bevan moved to Shipton Harbor then."

Interesting. He'd only gotten in because my aunt had declined.

Lorelai sighed again. "Of course, now, we hold to the traditional thirteen. If all three of you wanted to join, we'd be in a pickle. Times change, you know, but a coven must have thirteen."

They'd invited me before Miriam died. "So, you're down two now? With the loss of Miriam?" I asked.

Lorelai started. "Well, dear, I suppose we're down three. I hadn't thought of that. We just now got organized after losing poor Doras Miller just after the New Year. She had a heart attack and passed away in her sleep. And Bill... Well, you know what happened with him, as you helped to uncover his killer."

I frowned and averted my eyes, hoping she wouldn't bring up the army of skeletons I'd raised in the cemetery. Those skeletons dragged the witch hunter, Carmen Moonflower, underground. I didn't know where they took her, but I had a feeling I was better off not knowing.

Lorelai added, "Penny isn't here tonight. She's not feeling well."

I raised my eyebrows. "I didn't even know Bill and Penny were a part of the coven."

"Oh, yes. Beloved, both of them. Of course, we invited Bill after your mother passed and you declined to join. We were trying to open ourselves to be more inclusive, and a necromancer certainly did that." She tittered behind her handkerchief before catching the eye of a woman across the room I vaguely remembered from visiting Yaya. "Excuse me, dear." She started to move away, then turned back to me, touching my hand. "Don't leave without saying goodbye."

Then in my head, she said, "*I need to discuss an urgent matter with you.*"

My eyes rounded, but I quickly schooled my reaction, because I got the feeling she didn't want anyone else to hear. She wouldn't have spoken directly in my head if she wanted the whole room to know. That didn't make me feel any more comfortable being there.

"How convenient they have three openings," I

whispered to Owen as he and Wallie closed in on me.

He shrugged. "Probably a coincidence."

Maybe. But someone killed Miriam and Larry and possibly my mom. I wasn't sure how her death fit into it all, but I was going to find out.

We mingled for a few more minutes. I found everyone pleasant except for a set of twins, Brandon and Ben Stamp. They were a quiet pair and mostly stayed to themselves. Whenever I glanced their way one of them, Brandon, I believed, glared at me. He didn't want me there. I didn't blame him; I didn't want me there either.

I found Wallie at the refreshment table with Owen. "Hey, I'm ready to roll but I have to say goodbye to Lorelai, so I'll meet you two in the car."

They nodded and headed out the door after a lot of goodbyes.

I turned just as Lorelai exited the library. I took that as my cue, so I followed her while trying not to be obvious about it.

Once in the foyer, she and CeCe moved toward me. CeCe smiled wide. "It was so good to see you. Thank you for coming." She looped an arm with mine and walked me outside as if seeing me off.

Lorelai stood on my other side. Once we

descended the steps, a warmth of magic surrounded us. I swallowed my panic. "What's going on?"

"I put a privacy circle around us so no one can hear what we are about to say." Lorelai glanced at CeCe.

The coven leader took my hands and spoke while smiling. I was betting she was doing it in case anyone was watching us. How did I know that? "We don't think Miriam's death was an accident."

Lorelai looked a little scared. "We can't trust anyone else in the coven with our speculations because there are too many things that don't add up."

Did they know about the coin in Mariam's pocket? I didn't think so because it wasn't in the news reports. Plus, Drew wouldn't make something like that public. Especially since Larry had confirmed it was the same one his murderer had used.

So, I didn't mention the coin to Lorelai or Cynthia. "What makes you think it wasn't an accident?"

Voices coming out from the foyer drew our attention to the twins. CeCe quickly said, "We can't talk here."

The circle of magic dropped from around us and

Lorelai drew me into a hug. "We have to get together for tea or wine sometime."

"That would be great." I had to find out what they knew. I glanced at the twins in the doorway and waved at them before getting into my car.

CHAPTER SEVEN

I didn't feel like shopping for dinner or cooking or anything. And I couldn't ask Alfred to cook every meal I didn't feel like preparing. Plus, he didn't even eat! Why on earth he insisted on preparing my meals was beyond me. Huh. Maybe he was poisoning me slowly.

I chuckled. Nah.

The weather didn't help to bring me out of my lazy mood. Rain had poured down all day, creating a miserable, soggy mess. Not to mention making it colder than it already was.

On the way home from my shift at the bookstore, I popped into the Mexican restaurant at the edge of town and put in an order for a veritable smorgasbord of food. It was just me and Owen tonight, but Olivia was supposed to come over and help me go through my grimoires, looking for anything that might help us send Luci back to Hell.

That was something I was betting wasn't going to be easy. I wasn't the type to give up on things once determination set in. And it has set. The devil needed to return to his kingdom.

I had called in the order right before I left work. It was a good thing because it seemed like I wasn't the only one who wanted take out. As I sat on a bench near the front, humming to myself and looking around at the artwork—and pretending not to smell the delicious aromas coming from the kitchen as my stomach growled like an angry creature, the front door opened. I turned to see who had come in and my heart stopped for a few beats and the pit of my stomach burned.

Drew walked in with a gorgeous woman on his arm.

She was younger than me. Thinner than me. And looked up at him like he'd hung the moon. My chest tightened while jealousy churned within.

"*Corium*," I whispered, waving my hand in front of my face, hoping Drew didn't sense the magic. If he did, would he know it was me? Crap on a cracker. I did the spell so that anyone who looked at me would find their eyes slipping past where I sat without noticing me there at all. It was like an invisibility spell, only I wasn't quite invisible, just easy to forget if someone looked hard enough.

"Two?" the hostess asked, and Drew nodded, the svelte woman still hanging onto his arm.

Shit. I couldn't be sure. It could've been someone from the police department. It could be an old girl-friend who he wasn't involved with anymore. Hell, it could've been his cousin or something. Plus, neither of us had said anything about exclusivity.

Then why in the seven Hades was my pulse hammering so fast?

We weren't like... engaged or anything! So we'd had one great date in Paris. So, we'd sat on the top of the Eiffel Tower together. That didn't mean he couldn't date other people.

So why was my blood boiling? And I wanted to yank all the hair out of her head? Whoa, I needed a drink and chill. I picked up my phone and texted Olivia.

Don't forget the wine.

She texted back instantly. **Already in my bag**.

The server came out of the kitchen with two big

bags. "Harper?" He looked around, then set the bags down on the counter and went back to the kitchen.

My pulse quickened again, and I searched the restaurant for Drew and his *date*. To my relief, they were seated far enough away that he couldn't have heard my name.

I'd already paid when I placed the order, so I snatched the bags up and ran out the door, nearly bowling right into a young couple as they reached for the door.

"What the hell?" the guy exclaimed. "I didn't feel any wind that would jerk the door open like that."

"Me, either," the girl said. "Creepy. Let's go somewhere else to eat."

Crap. Crap. I scurried to my car and bent down behind it, getting soaked by the heavy rain. "*Revelare.*" Visible again, I straightened up and put the food on the back floorboard. It wouldn't be good if someone saw my car driving itself down the road. Although that would be a good reason to have a dash-cam. Playback people's reaction to a driverless car. Might make some good money if it went viral. I snorted at my thoughts. I really have lost it.

Olivia was already there when I got home. She rushed out to grab one of the bags from me while holding a large umbrella. It was impressive. Like family size. "That's a big umbrella."

She grinned. "I know, right? I found it a craft fair my mom and I went to a few years ago." She watched me from the corner of her eye as we hustled inside my house and put the food on the coffee table. "What's wrong?"

I straightened and pretended to play dumb. "Besides being soaked? Nothing. I'm going to get out of these wet clothes. Can you get some plates and glasses? I'll let Owen know to come down and get food."

I rushed up the stairs, sloshing away before she could call me out on the nothing comment. I planned to tell her, just not until I was in dry, comfy clothes. And with an enormous glass of wine.

Sporting my neon pink flannel sleep pants and a black tee that said, "What's up, Witches," I headed down the hall. I yelled to Owen when I got to the top of the stairs. "Dinner is on the coffee table."

By the time I got downstairs, Owen was fixing a plate. Wow, that was impressive. "Did you learn to teleport? Because that would be cool."

Owen straightened and frown lines formed on his forehead. After a few moments, he laughed. "No. I was already down here when you yelled for me."

Oh, that made more sense. But I was a little disappointed that necromancers couldn't teleport. Imagine the gas you'd save.

He'd recently started working at the bookstore, too. I'd been writing more since moving here, and my book sales were picking up, meaning I didn't have to take on as many shifts. The house was paid for, so all I had was electricity, water, and the internet. I didn't watch much TV, so didn't bother with cable. I did have a few streaming subscriptions from when Wallie lived at home in Philly. Alfred and Larry had been enjoying them.

"Are you hanging out with us tonight? We're going to start the search for a way to send Luci back." Olivia asked.

He held up his plate. "After I eat, I might."

When he walked off, I grabbed a plate and loaded it up.

With a snap of his fingers, Owen whirled to face me. "That's what I meant to tell you. I convinced Cliff to let me put in an occult section so we can order books that are relevant to the witches in the area. Real, good books. Not Paranormal fiction."

That was a great idea. "Spot on, Owen, wonderful. He was cool with it?"

He shrugged. "Well, he thinks it's for Wiccans,

which some of them will be. But I don't think he knows there are more than that sort of spiritual witch around."

"Good." I threw out our trash. "Let's keep it that way."

Once we were alone, I tried to ignore Olivia as she stared at me. It was difficult because she was worse than Snooze when he wanted something.

I had a fork full of rice halfway to my mouth when she said, "Come on, spill it."

I locked gazes with her and shoved the rice in my mouth. Then chewed very slowly. That only earned me a throw pillow upside the head. I started laughing, which made me choke on the rice.

Alfred rushed down the stairs, and I waved him off. "I'm fine."

Larry stuck his head over the railing. Thanks to the gods, it stayed attached to his body. "You're choking. Do you need the Heimlich?"

"No!" My voice squeaked as I yelled the word. Then I calmed and said softer, "No, thank you for your concern."

The thought of Larry's boney fist on my chest sent a shiver through me. Not in this lifetime. Or the next.

"What is it?" Olivia insisted again.

"Could you imagine the skeleton giving you the Heimlich? No way will his boney hands be anywhere near the girls." I made a circular motion over my breasts as I shuddered.

Olivia giggled, which turned into a full laugh as she fell to her side on the couch and rolled to the floor.

It took her a good ten minutes to recover. She sat up and remained on the floor but still didn't let me off the hook. "What is bothering you?"

"What makes you think anything is bothering me?" I took another big bite.

"Because your eyes are greener than normal. That means your magic is close to the surface, right?"

Well, look who'd been doing some witchy home-work. "It does," I mumbled around my food.

Damn, most witches' magic was tied closely to their emotions. Now that mine ran free inside me because I was no longer suppressing either side of my powers, my emotions at seeing Drew with that woman had struck all of my nerves. And my magic.

After taking a drink of my soda, I told her about Drew. "...So, anyway, I have no proof that it was any sort of date. But Liv, you should've seen the way she looked at him."

Olivia took a bite of refried beans and then

pointed her fork at me. "I'm going to string him up by his balls."

"Olivia! You'll do no such thing. Especially before we figure out who she was." If anyone was going to be stringing up balls, it would be me. But I wouldn't.

She scowled at me. "You're no fun."

I snorted and took a big bite of burrito. "I'm a blast. But I'm not going to castrate Drew because he knows another woman." Or had dinner with her. It was just food. I'd keep telling myself that until I got a chance to ask him about her.

She sniffed but didn't press it. "I'm sure you're right," she said. "She's probably his therapist or something. She helps him suppress his violent urge to murder his new girlfriend for being a witch."

"That's totally it." I let sarcasm leak into the words. Then added an eye roll for visual effect.

Olivia and I finished our dinner and cleaned up our mess in the living room, which we'd converted to a sort-of library. All the books that had been scattered on shelves all over the house now resided on the built-ins here in the living room where previously they'd been full of knick-knacks that were boxed in the attic. Most of them had been precious to Yaya or Winnie but didn't mean a lot to me. I hadn't been able to get rid of them but didn't need them displayed, either.

"Okay, so we're pretty much just going through all these old books, looking for any hint of a spell that could be used or adapted to help us send Luci back," I said. "Just grab a grimoire and start reading."

Owen was still eating in the kitchen. But Alfred wandered in with Larry in tow. "We can help," Larry said. "I can't turn pages well, but Alfred can, and we can both read."

I handed them a book. "We'll take all the help we can get, but why don't you two stick to the newer books that aren't as valuable, just in case?"

I had really ancient ones in the attic somewhere. We'd have to search for them if none of the ones down here panned out.

Alfred nodded once and took the book to the desk in the corner where he and Larry got to work. Snooze wandered in and stretched out across the desk a few minutes later, forcing them to pull the book back and give him room.

"Bad kitty," I whispered as Snooze's tail twitched and he opened one eye to stare at me. "Yeah, I'm talking to you." Crazy cat.

About an hour after we dug into searching the

grimoires, Oliva squeaked and yelled, "I found something!"

I jerked my gaze to her and waited while she read over the page. She sagged back into the oversized chair she'd moved to a few minutes ago and her face scrunched up. "Never mind. That's not it."

I sighed and went back to my search. We had a few more false hope outbursts over the next few hours. I tossed my head back against the sofa and groaned. "There has to be a spell for finding a spell. Like a magical internet search for grimoires."

Owen chuckled. "There might be. It just comes down to finding the right spell to suit your purpose."

"That doesn't help." I laughed, then let out a dramatic breath and focused on the book in my lap.

Wallie nudged me while placing his grimoire on top of mine. He pointed to the page. "Will this work?"

The title of the spell was "Get rid of unwanted evil," and I snorted.

"That is exactly what I want to do." I studied the incantation and ingredients. It was more of an evil-spirit banishing spell, but I bet I could tweak it to include a demon. Demons were kind of like spirits. And my new neighbor was the king of evil.

"Nope. That won't work."

The sound of a male's low whisper in my ear made me jump a foot off the couch, spilling the books on the floor. I whirled around with my hand raised. My magic instantly flowed into my palms, ready to blast the man at my command.

I narrowed my eyes and called the magic back. "You need to learn to knock."

Luci straightened from where he leaned against the back of the sofa. How long had he been there reading over my shoulder? *Without* me sensing him?

He waved his hand and the book with the evil spirit banishing spell floated over to him. Opening to the page with the spell, he shook his head. "This won't work."

Stepping forward, I snatched the book from him. "Not the way it's written. I'll modify it and make it work."

He disappeared and reappeared directly in front of me. I gasped and fought the urge to run. I could talk the crap, but when it came to backing up my sass with the devil, I was chicken.

Pathetic.

A slow, wicked smile formed, and he leaned closer. "You could just accept the fact that I like your little town, and I'm here to stay."

"Not today, Satan." I pushed past him to put

some space between us. "You are a menace and don't belong here."

That reminded me, I also needed to make anti-compulsion charms for my family and friends. Myself included.

When I got a few feet from him, I turned and asked, "If you're so smart, how do we get rid of you?"

He laughed. Out loud. "My dear, Ava. If I told you that, it wouldn't be any fun watching you try to find out."

Then he dematerialized.

Damn demon.

CHAPTER EIGHT

*D*ancing around the book stacks, I dusted and bopped to the tune blaring from the radio up front. I was the only one that didn't mind dusting; Owen and Clint hated it. Plus, I'd honed my cleaning spell, so the dust danced in front of me at ground level, as we worked our way toward the back door. I just had to make sure to do it when Clint wasn't here.

My boss didn't know about magic. At least I didn't think he did. I wasn't going to be the one to tell him either.

"Love me all niiiiiii—" I cut off abruptly as my alarm went off, the magic from the spell nipping at my skin.

Magic was a handy thing. Owen and I had rigged

an alarm that beeped loudly whenever anyone entered the store. The catch was that only he and I could hear it.

As I said. Handy.

Sure, there was a bell on the door that Clint could hear, but Owen and I had wanted something that went off the moment someone touched the door. It gave us that second or two to check out the energy of the person coming in and hide our spells and magic if we needed to.

We couldn't be too careful since Owen had been kidnapped and almost killed last October by a crazy witch hunter. We weren't taking any chances. Necromancers had a bad rep, plus, I was supposed to be this all-powerful necro-witch hybrid. So far, I wasn't all *that* powerful. The jury was still out on whether or not I was all that special.

At the sound of the magical alarm, the dust dropped to the floor, scattering under the stacks as it had been instructed to do.

The dust could hear the alarm too, because why not?

"Hey," Clint said. "Was that you caterwauling?"

Clint was thin and about four inches taller than me with tanned skin that I didn't know was real or from a can. His gray eyes twinkled, telling me he was teasing me with his comment.

I put one hand on my hips and shook the feather duster at him. "Hey, now. I can't be good at everything."

He chuckled, but something told me he was questioning my sanity. There were days that I questioned it too.

I had to be careful around him and probably warn Owen to be. Clint was a good guy, but I didn't need to deal with explaining all this mess to him. He was, as far as I knew, fully human. It would be tricky.

"How goes it?" I asked. "Oh, did you approve the occult section?" I glanced his way, trying to sound casual as I kept dusting without the aid of the spell.

"Yes, I did. I need to order the books," he called.

Since his voice drifted out from the back room, I twirled my finger and grabbed up all the dust I'd been accumulating, coaxing it out from under the stacks. "Come on," I muttered. "Quickly." Scurrying backward, I snatched up the small trash bin and hid between the stacks, still swirling my finger. The dust rose in a tornado.

"Do you know anything about this stuff?"

This time, Clint's voice came from much closer. Crap.

I pointed into the bin and cut off the spell. The dust fell, most of it hitting the trash can liner. Stepping forward, I shook the can a bit to get the dust to settle. "Sure," I said. "I'd be happy to put in the order for you."

Walking out of the stacks, I nearly stepped right into Clint. I jumped and swallowed a scream. He furrowed his brow at the trash can. "I thought you were dusting?"

"There was a lot of dust on one of those shelves." I laughed nervously and changed the subject. "Show me the ordering system?"

He looked skeptical but turned toward the front counter with the laptop in his hands. He must've brought it out of his office before scaring me to death.

A few minutes after I sat down and started browsing the options, Clint got bored and left me to it. Good.

I was anything but bored and had to make myself stop browsing and shopping before I spent all of the bookstore's money. "Okay, Clint I made a big order, but I'm going to buy several of these as soon as you get them in," I called. "And it's time for me to go!"

He sauntered out of his office with a smile on his face. "So, you're into these occult books, huh?"

"Yeah." I nodded, hoping to look innocent. "They're great research for my novels."

With my bag on my shoulder, I started toward the door, but as soon as I looked at the glass, I stopped. "I forgot about all this rain," I said with a sigh. "I love rain, but enough is enough."

It'd been pouring off and on for the last several days. I was so over it.

Clint chuckled. "Here." He handed me my umbrella, which I'd almost forgotten. "Have fun swimming home!"

"It would be a lot more fun if it wasn't so cold." I waved and opened the umbrella, needing it even though my car was only like ten feet away.

As soon as I shook it off and managed to shut my car door, I sighed. The act of closing it and shaking it off had me nearly as dang wet as I would've been if I'd just rushed to the car without the stupid thing.

Shivering, I cranked up the heat just as my phone blared the ringtone that Olivia had set for her contact when I wasn't paying attention. *Witchy Woman* blared from the device and it had me cracking up. So forever now, when Olivia called, it was with that song, plus a picture I'd sneakily taken of her when she wasn't looking. She'd been picking something out of her teeth.

She'd also set my home phone line to ring on my cell as *Monster Mash*, which with the menagerie at my place, I'd also left that one on there. It fit our lives at the moment.

"What's up, frand?" I answered.

"Another death," she replied in a hushed tone and my heart sank. "And Sam said if we hurry, we can check out the scene so you can do your thing."

"No way," I replied, also whispering. "I mean, yes, to doing my thing. No way in that I can't believe there's been another death." I paused, then asked, "Why am I whispering?"

"I don't know," she hissed, then laughed although it didn't sound as happy as her normal laugh did. "I don't know why I am either!"

"Okay, where is it? Who was it? I just left the bookstore." I didn't pull out until she told me where I should go.

"I don't know this person," she said. "It was at her house on Beaver Drive."

I snickered. "I love that street name."

"Me too." She chuckled along with me. "Beaver."

"Okay, okay. What was the person's name?" I asked. We were too giggly when there'd been a murder.

"Um, Lorelai Fontinell."

My heart sank to my feet while sadness churned in the pit of my soul. "No," I began whispering again. "She's a member of the coven."

"You're joking."

"I'm not."

With a heavy heart, I put the phone on speaker and the car in reverse. "Are you on your way?"

"Almost there," she replied.

"I'll meet you there." I hung up and swiped tears away as I headed to the other side of town.

Lorelai had been so nice to me at the Coven meeting. She'd made me want to consider joining. She also had information about Mariam's so-called accident. Something or someone was causing them. But why and how?

I pulled up behind Olivia's 4-Runner and brushed the tears from my cheeks. I was getting sick and damn tired of finding dead witches.

Olivia jumped out of her car and hurried to open my car door. "Come on and leave the umbrella."

"Why?" I asked as I burrowed my face into my jacket to avoid the freezing rain.

"You'll see."

Uh oh. I didn't like the sound of that. Or the look of horror and disgust that briefly flashed across Olivia's face.

Sam stood in the front doorway. Luckily for us, Lorelai's house had a nice, deep porch to shield us from the rain. He put one hand on my arm and one on Olivia's. "Brace yourselves," he said. "It's bad."

I sucked in a deep breath and closed my eyes, opening them when I felt Sam move out of the way.

Olivia gasped and I wanted to, but the shock was too much. It hurt my heart.

Gore and gross things were quickly becoming a way of life, considering I was a necromancer.

"Is anyone here?" I whispered.

"No," Sam said. "The coroner just left. We're alone for now but he'll be back in an hour for the body." He arched an eyebrow. "It took some fancy talk for him to leave without her."

"Did you find anything on her?" I asked.

He nodded and checked his notes. "Yep. A coin."

The same one that was left on Miriam and Larry, I bet.

I walked carefully around the body of what might have become my friend. "Can you remove the umbrella yet?" I asked as I stared down at what I could see of Lorelai.

A small, black umbrella covered most of her. Squatting down, I looked underneath to see if what I suspected was what happened.

Yep.

The pointy end of the umbrella protruded from Lorelai's eye.

Damn it.

I tried not to breathe. Not sure why because she didn't stink yet. One would think that as a necromancer, I'd be used to seeing the dead.

I was not. I'd avoided it at all costs until a few months ago.

"I guess," Sam said. "We're ruling it an accident, so there won't be much in the way of forensics."

I glanced up at him. "The coin is a link to Miriam's 'accident'." I used air quotes to make my point.

He shrugged. "If that truly is the case then it is a supernatural cause of death that the humans don't need to know about. So it's ruled accidental, for now.

I nodded. That made sense, sort of. For now. "Okay. Remove it."

He put on gloves and reached for the handle. It came out of her eye socket with a sickening squelch sound.

Olivia gasped and covered her face, then turned her back.

"Time of death?" I asked.

"Sometime yesterday between noon and two," he said.

"Okay. I think I can get her to talk without too much magic or disturbing things too much."

I studied Lorelai for a long while, noticing her blackened witch's mark shining from her chest, just visible above the collar of her shirt.

Sucking in a deep breath, I closed my eyes and called on the magic Owen and I had been working on. To animate a corpse partially and not have them jumping up and running around town. I just wanted Lorelai to tell me how this happened.

I sent barely a sliver of magic toward her while concentrating on Lorelai's brain and vocal cords, trying to animate just her head and upper chest area.

"Lorelai, how did you die?" I whispered, leaning close. If I did this right, she wouldn't speak loudly, and I'd have to strain to hear.

Scaring the crap out of me, Lorelai sat up suddenly, her blonde hair matted with the blood that had drained from her eye socket. I scrambled backward, deeper into the house as Sam and Olivia retreated onto the porch to watch in horror. "This isn't me. That's not my magic," I squeaked as I jerked the small bit of my magic away from the corpse.

"Keep your magic away from the witch, necromancer," Lorelai's pale lips said as her head turned all the way around to stare at me with one milky eye. "Let the dead lie."

Her body relaxed and fell back on the ground, landing in the exact same spot it had been in before I tried to raise her.

"Shit," I whispered, rapidly shaking my hands as if to shake off the bad juju. "Shit, *shit*."

"What the hell was that?" Olivia screeched from the front porch.

Sam peered around the corner with his gun pointed at Lorelai's body and Olivia peeked around the other side of the door. "Is it safe?" she asked.

"It's safe," I said. "Sometimes witches put spells on themselves so that when they die, they'll stay dead. They don't want their bodies used by dark necromancers." Not that I'd ever use that kind of magic. It took a real sicko for that. That's how Alfreds were created, but ghouls didn't normally end up benevolent chefs like mine. "But that also means we can't use her body to get answers about her death."

Feeling like a failure for not being able to get a lead on how the two accidents could happen and why, I moved to the front door where Sam and Olivia still waited, eyeing Lorelai's body as if it was going to jump up again. "Can I see the coin?"

Without looking away from the body, Sam pulled a small bag from his pocket with the coin inside. I took it and studied it. "It's the same one found on Mariam. Larry says it's also the same as the one that was placed in his pocket moments before he died."

"Yeah. But we don't have Larry's." Sam frowned. "And we can't use him as a source."

I knew that. No one would believe that a skeleton claimed to die in an accident while having a coin in his pocket.

When I started to open the baggie, Sam covered my hand. "Don't touch it. We need to take prints... you know, off the record."

Nodding, I said, "I wasn't going to touch it. I'm checking for magic." But there wasn't anything lingering. This was the freshest coin I'd been able to examine.

He took it from me after putting on a glove and then dumped the coin out of the bag into his palm. Ah, that was better. I hovered my hand over it, feeling the charge of dark power. Just as we feared, the coin was cursed. I just didn't know how or by whom. Without that information, I didn't know how to uncurse it. Or protect other witches from suffering the same fate.

"After you check it for prints off the record, can I have it? I might be able to do a locator spell or some other kind to find who the owner is."

Sam nodded. "Yeah, sure."

And I was out. I couldn't take being in the same room with Lorelai's corpse any longer. The whole anti-necromancer spell was a shock, and it had freaked me the heck out.

CHAPTER NINE

"*S*nooze, stop it."

Mr. Snoozerton lay behind me, randomly scratching my butt with his back feet. He wanted my attention, or he wanted food. It was hard to tell with him at times. I'd swat him off, then a few minutes later, he'd do it again.

"I'm not playing right now, Snooze!" I turned and laughed when I found him splayed out on his back, showing his big, fluffy belly for pets. "I love petting your super curly belly hair, Snoozer, but I'm busy." I gave him a quick pat on the tummy then turned back to the trunk.

Alfred shuffled over and glared down at the big, rotten cat.

"I swear, the only thing we're going to find up

here is a bunch of dust," Olivia said as Alfred and Snooze had a staring contest. She glanced at the two, frowned, then shook her head.

Alfred grunted and Snooze rolled over the other way, taking his claws with him. "Thanks, Alfie," I said, still marveling at the power the ghoul had over that insane cat. "I can fix that," I replied to Olivia about the dust, not the attention-whore of a cat. There was no help for him.

I had already fixed him when he died as a kitten. I ended up turning him immortal somehow. That crazy cat was going to outlive us all. I shot Olivia an alarming look that made her sit up straight. "What's wrong?"

"I just realized that Snooze will outlive me."

Her eyes got big. "You need to find him a god-parent or something just in case."

Yeah, but who could I trust with my big furry baby? "Wallie can take him and then pass him down the family."

Olivia snorted. "He's not a family heirloom."

I gasped in mock surprise that she would say such a thing. "He is too! A precious heirloom."

"Precious is right." Olivia giggled and then motioned to all the dust.

Oh, yeah. I was supposed to fix it.

Doing my finger twirl, I gathered up the dust and sent it out of the small vent in the corner of the attic. "There. Better?"

Olivia nodded and opened another box. "Perfect, thanks. How much would you charge to come to do that to my entire house once a week?"

"Remind me, and I'll do it every time I come over, free of charge." I was supposed to be super powerful, yet I used my magic to clean the house more than anything.

Sam and Olivia tended to come here more than I went there, though. With all the myriad of creatures living here, I liked to be around as much as possible to supervise things. Alfred was a pretty stern babysitter, but still, he was a ghoul.

"Nothing in this box either." Olivia sighed and rocked back on her heels. "Are you sure there are more grimoires up here?"

"I thought there were," I said. "The really old ones that we had copied into new books and didn't want to disturb anymore."

"If you copied them, why are we looking for them?" Larry asked.

"Because I'm desperate," I snapped. With a sigh, I relaxed and closed the trunk. "I'm sorry. I didn't mean to bite your head off."

Olivia snorted, then quickly covered her mouth, and looked at the skeleton in horror.

His head had an unfortunate tendency to fall off.

I bit back my laughter and avoided looking at Olivia at all costs. The last thing I needed was to get a glimpse of her laugh-strangled face and burst out giggling myself.

We were no closer to finding Larry's killer than we'd been the day he'd turned up on my porch. I didn't want to make him think we weren't taking this seriously.

The truth was, we'd been doing spells and the police department was doing everything it could as well. Sam and Drew had even snuck one of the coins to us to spell. Nothing Owen or I had tried gave any results. Whoever was using these coins was covering their tracks too well with their own spell work.

It was going to take some old-fashioned sleuthing to get to the bottom of this mystery.

And in the meantime, I had to figure out how to get Lucifer to go back to Hell without taking all of us with him. Some of the books I'd ordered for Clint had descriptions that had made me hopeful that they'd have something helpful inside. We'd find out when they arrived.

Olivia had scoured the online book world for

occult books, but apparently, witches hadn't gone electronic yet. There was a stunning shortage of authentic occult eBooks.

As I opened another trunk, I considered the possibility of turning some of my family's grimoires and books electronic. But I'd have to figure out a way to make them seem like fiction to the humans.

Could I put a spell on the internet?

This was the sort of thing I'd like to discuss with a coven, but they had to be total assholes. I supposed I could call Cynthia. We hadn't yet had our talk about Mariam's accident. And now Lorelai's.

"Here's something," Larry said. "This box has books."

I hurried over to the corner to peer down into the crate Larry had just opened. "This is it," I said excitedly. "Thank you."

Turning, I carried it to the small table against the wall to go through it. If I sat one more minute on the hard attic floor, my back would revolt against me. It was already trying to.

I stepped over Snoozle, who was sniffing around the floor. "There's nothing there, Snoozer."

He chuffed at me, looking up with his little tongue barely sticking out.

"You've got a blep," I told him. "In case you didn't know."

The old meanie shot me a glare, then delicately licked his front paw, as if he'd meant to have his tongue sticking out the whole time.

I shook my head and went back to inspecting the contents of the box. As I pulled out the first book, carefully opening it, Snoozer walked toward the back of the attic.

Olivia sat in the other chair and grabbed a book, too.

When Alfred and Larry came closer, I held up my hand. "Olivia and I will handle these. Thanks, guys." I appreciated their help, but we didn't need their dry and bony fingers ripping pages.

Snooze meowed a couple of times from the corner as Olivia and I slowly read through each of the grimoires. I had no idea what the cat was doing, so I ignored him. He sometimes meowed at Winston, the house. At least I hoped Winston was the house itself and not a ghost. I wasn't ready for them yet.

I'd gotten to the third book when a racket scared me to death. I jumped in my seat, almost dropping the grimoire.

Snoozle was howling something fierce, but when

I rushed over to the back of the attic, he was nowhere to be found.

"Snoozer!" I yelled.

He went silent for a second, then yowled again, and I could've sworn it sounded like the word help.

"Where are you?" Olivia called from right behind me.

Snooze yowled again, and Alfred dropped to his knees beside me, scrabbling at the wooden planks of the floor.

I ran to the corner, to an old box of tools, looking for a hammer. There wasn't a hammer in the box, but there was a crowbar. It would do!

Returning to the other side of the attic and my pitiful cat who was still crying and howling at the top of his lungs, I wedged the crowbar between the planks of wood and pressed down on the end to try to loosen them.

Snoozer went quiet, then yowled again, and I paused, looking at Olivia. "Did he just tell me to hurry?"

"It sure sounded like it," she muttered. "That cat is something else."

I heaved against the crowbar, and the plank came up on one end with an awful squeal.

Snooze's head wedged out of the small space I'd

created with the crowbar. "Snooze, wait," I cried. "I don't have it fully up yet!"

Leaning against the crowbar, I held the plank up as long as I could while Snooze wiggled his way out of the hole. "How did you get in there?" I yelled when he finally got free, then shot across the attic. I turned my head to see his tail disappear out the door.

"Wait," Olivia said. She reached carefully into the hole while I tried to use the crowbar to hold the plank steady. "There's something here."

She pulled out something wrapped in an old, ratty towel, then peered down in the hole again. "Hang on."

Reaching into her back pocket, she pulled out her phone, then turned on the flashlight on it. After a careful examination, she shook her head. "That's all. Let it go."

"How in the world did he get under there?" I asked, letting the plank fall back into place.

I stood and stepped on the floor. Nothing. No sound and no movement. None of the planks nearby were loose either. Olivia knocked on walls and the floor around the area. We didn't find anything that told us how the fat cat got under the floor.

"Was it the house?" Olivia asked as she wiped a bead of sweat from her forehead. We'd looked everywhere. There was no way we could find that Snooze could've gotten under the floorboards.

"I don't see what else it could've been. Winston up to mischief again."

As if agreeing with me, the shutters on the front of the house rattled in the wind. "Yep, it was him."

I returned to the table and took the towel-wrapped mystery from Alfred. "Let's see what Snoozer accidentally found. Whatever it is, Winston really wanted us to have it."

CHAPTER TEN

"It's a mirror," I whispered. Why in the heck would a mirror be hiding in the floor of the attic? Apparently, Winston knew, or the dang house wouldn't have trapped poor Snooze in the hollow spot with the mirror.

Winston and I were going to have a serious talk about his attitude.

"Hey, what are you guys up to?" Owen said. "I heard a racket." He stuck his head in the attic door and looked around. "Everything okay?"

I shook my head. "We think the house is acting up again. Snooze got caught under the floorboards and we had to fight to get him out." I sat back and looked at Owen. "And now that I think about it, I'm wondering if the house wasn't fighting me a little."

Definitely having a talk with Winston. His behavior was unacceptable.

"Why would it trap the silly cat, then fight you to get him out?" Olivia asked. "I think the house wanted you to find whatever's in that towel."

I shrugged and picked up the mirror. "Let's see." A beautiful, antique hand mirror. The silver handle and frame holding in the mirror looked to be hand-carved with floral-like designs. Going by the weight and the magic that kissed at my fingers and hand, it was cast from real silver. Would have to be to have a spell on it.

"I don't remember ever seeing this before," I said. "Why was it hidden?"

Owen held out his hand. "May I?"

I nodded and handed the mirror over. Owen closed his eyes and held it, then smelled it, then peered closely at the reflective surface before turning it over and licking it.

Ew! "Why'd you do that?"

He wiped off the back with his sleeve and gave it back. "Some magic tastes bitter. Try touching it with the tiniest bit of magic," he suggested.

I eyed him suspiciously. He knew something, but like the good teacher he was, he wanted me to discover the secret on my own. Fine. Whatever.

With a shrug, I took it and did as he said, drawing out my magic and picturing it as a single strand of hair glancing up against the mirror's surface.

To my shock, the mirror blazed to life, light coming out of the glass like it had a freaking hundred-watt bulb behind it.

"What the frack?" Olivia squawked.

We all peered into the glass. "If we get sucked into this mirror," I whispered. "I swear..."

I had too much stuff to do to be lost inside a magical mirror. I had a killer to find and a sheriff to seduce. Wait... I had no idea where that last thought came from. But it sounded fun. It's been a *long* time since I wasn't responsible for my own orgasm.

Filing the seduction of the sheriff away for later, I studied the mirror again.

A voice came from the glass, which no longer held my reflection, I belatedly realized. "Who's there?"

I gasped and my heart jumped in my chest. I knew that voice. "Yaya?" I whispered as tears filled my eyes. "Is that you?"

My sweet Yaya's face appeared in the reflection of the mirror. Her olive-toned skin was as flawless as it had been before she died. There were only a few fine lines around her eyes, mouth, and forehead.

Yaya had been the master of looking young. She'd always told me it was good genes. I had told her it was that *and* a little magic.

Yaya's bright green eyes lit up. "Oh, my goodness. Ava. You're all grown up."

"How are you in this mirror?" I cried. "Are you real?"

My chest tightened and my heart ached to hug her.

She shook her head. "In a way. I'm an imprint."

I'd read somewhere about imprints. "So you have the knowledge and personality of Yaya up until the moment she put you in this mirror."

She nodded. "Exactly." Her gaze shifted behind me. "Who are your friends?"

"This is Olivia," I said. "She's my best friend."

Olivia stuck her head over my shoulder. "It's a pleasure to meet you, ma'am. I've heard so much about you."

"And this is Owen, he's been teaching me necromancy." I twisted the mirror so Owen could wave.

He smiled nervously. "It's a real honor to meet even the imprint of the famous Yaya."

My grandmother tittered. "I'm happy to meet you all, but Ava, honey, we don't have much time. An imprint only lasts so long. When you pull back your magic, the mirror will go dark. You'll be able to see the imprint again as long as the magic I imbibed in it lasts, but I can't tell when it will fade until it happens."

"How long do they usually last?" I asked.

Owen answered. "It varies and depends on the strength of the witch that cast the imprint. Generally several hours."

"Okay," I said. "You won't be like... lonely or anything when I'm not talking to you, right?"

"No, sweet girl. It's sort of like I sleep. When I made this mirror, you were just a teenager. And now look at you." Her eyes softened. "You're just beautiful."

My bottom lip trembled slightly. "Not as beautiful as you."

As much as I wanted to spend hours catching you with Yaya, I didn't have that much time. But I did spare a few minutes to tell her the short version of my life. "Clay and I ran off to Philly after our wedding. We had a beautiful baby boy, Wallace Clayton. We call him Wallie, who is not a baby anymore. He's going to Harvard to be a doctor. My Clay...he died in a car crash a little over five years ago."

"Oh, sweetheart, I'm so sorry. I know how much you loved that boy."

We were silent for a few seconds, just staring at one another before Yaya asked, "Darling, is there anything you need to ask me? I have all the memories and knowledge up until this point in my life."

I shook my head and smiled. "No, Yaya, I'm just so glad to see you."

"Yes," Olivia said. "We do!"

I looked over my shoulder at her, frowning. "What?"

"Ask her about your mom's death," she said.

Well, duh. I wanted to slap my forehead. "Oh, Yaya, yes. Was there any suspicion that my mother could've been murdered?" I asked.

Yaya winced. "I always had a feeling of it. But I never had anything more than that. No proof, not even a hint of a spell."

"What about a coin?" I asked. "Was there a strange coin in her pocket?"

Yaya's eyes widened. "As a matter of fact, there was. It's in my jewelry box, dear one. I kept it."

I nodded. Feelings of dread, sorrow, and hope for being closer to finding the killer swirled inside me. "Okay, Yaya. Thank you. I'll check it. If I have more questions, I'll contact you again, but I'm going to let you go for now so that there will be plenty of time for Wallie to meet you, okay?"

She smiled and leaned closer to her side of the mirror. "I love you, my Ava girl. I'm so proud of the woman you've become."

With a sniffle, I pulled the thread of magic back into me and collapsed against Olivia as I cried. My Yaya.

"She had to have made this not long before she died," I whispered. "She died when I was nineteen." It was the year before Clay and I got married.

Once the mirror went dark, I wrapped it back in the cloth we found it in. Glancing at Owen, I asked, "Can you grab that box of grimoires and take them to the living room? I'm going to find a safe place for the mirror and search for that coin in Yaya's jewelry box."

I kept that jewelry box in my room on the top shelf of my bookcase. I never opened it because I didn't want to grieve anymore loved ones at the moment.

"Sure." Owen picked up the books on the table and added them to the box before lifting it in his arms.

Olivia and I followed him down with Alfred and Larry right behind us. The attic stairs ended on the second floor at the end of the hall on the side where my room was, so I darted inside while the guys continued to the first floor. It was close to dinner time, so I figured Alfred and Larry would be starting dinner. I'd told them I could call for delivery, but they'd argued with me.

I opened the top drawer of my dresser and set the mirror inside. Olivia came in and sat on my bed. "Are you okay?"

I glanced at her and nodded. "It was great seeing her, even though it wasn't really her."

Moving to my bookcase, I lifted my hands and pushed out magic to lift the jewelry box from its high perch and bring it down to me. I moved to the bed and sat with one leg bent in front of me and the other draped over the side. Olivia turned to face me, mirroring my pose.

Neither one of us spoke as I searched each drawer of the box until I found the coin. My heart thumped crazily loud in my ears and my hands shook as I pulled out the coin. If this matched the one found on Mariam and Lorelai, it would confirm my mother had been killed by the same curse placed on each of the coins.

My heartbeat froze as I stared at it. "It's the

same," I breathed, holding out the coin for Olivia to see.

"I'm so sorry." Olivia placed her hand on my arm. "We'll find out who did this."

Damn straight we would.

"Is that coin going to kill us?"

I snapped my gaze to Olivia's very worried look. "No. There is no magic left in this coin. If Yaya didn't feel any in it when *she* found it, then I'm guessing the curse is a one-time use deal. Once it did what it was intended, then the coin is just a coin."

"That makes sense." She hesitated. "How'd you feel magic on the one at Lorelai's then?"

"I'm guessing Yaya didn't get this one until a while after Mom died. Probably the hospital or funeral home returned it to us. But to be safe, I'll take this downstairs to the conservatory to douse it in saltwater. Neutralize any magic left in the silver." I waved my hand and the box floated back to its home on the top shelf of the bookcase.

When we reached the bottom floor, a knock sounded on the door. Olivia and I glanced at each other, and I stuffed the coin in my pocket and answered the door. No one was there, and I got a feeling of deja vu. Then, an envelope floated inside and stopped inches from my face. Yep, definitely been here before.

I plucked the coven letter out of the air and closed the door, then went through the kitchen to the conservatory. Setting the letter on my workstation while I filled a glass bowl with water and dumped salt into it. Once the bowl was full and salt mixed in, I dropped the coin inside. A puff of dark grey smoke shot up from the water.

"What was that? Please tell me it's not Satan's evil twin or anyone else." Olivia backed toward the door.

I snorted. "No. That was the last tiny bit of magic that was hidden inside the coin."

"Ah. Freaky."

Picking up the letter, I turned to press my back against the counter. I *so* didn't want to go to another meeting. But I had to play nice with the coven if I wanted to figure out who was behind the cursed coins.

"Are you going to open it or stare at it?"

"I don't know, I thought I could try to read it while still in the envelope." I tore the seal and pulled out the letter. My frown deepened as I read.

"Well?" Olivia prompted.

"Wallie, Owen, and I have been invited to a

coven party. The dress is formal." I tossed the letter on the counter and sighed. "I don't want to go."

"But you have to for the sole reason that I *can't* go. You need to live the experience for me, then give me a play by play of the night." She grinned and batted her lashes. "Oh, are you taking Drew?"

"What? No."

"Why?"

I stared at her for a moment. "Because he's a born hunter. I'm pretty sure that would be frowned upon."

Olivia laughed. "It would be funny to see their faces if he showed."

The thought *was* tempting but I couldn't put Drew through the torture of mingling with witches. Heck, I didn't even want to mingle with witches.

However, I couldn't turn down the invite because I had info to fish for.

CHAPTER ELEVEN

"Hey, thanks for coming!" I opened the door wide and stepped back so CeCe could come in. "I appreciate it."

"No problem. I don't mind helping a new witch with her protection spells." CeCe walked in with a big smile on her face. "Even if you're not a totally new witch, I know you're learning a lot right now."

I twisted my hands together after I closed the door. "Hang on."

Gathering my power, I spread it over the house, creating a barrier. Not a ward, anyone could come through it. But as long as the person wasn't under the barrier, they couldn't hear anything that went on in the house. "There. Nobody can hear us now."

CeCe's eyebrows flew up. "Is this not a bit of training?"

I shook my head and smiled ruefully at her. "I need some help with something kind of major that I'd rather not have the whole town knowing."

She nodded as we walked into the living room. We sat and Alfred walked in with a tray and tea. He grunted as he set it down. CeCe's eyes twinkled. "Thank you, sir."

Alfred nodded his stiff neck and backed out of the room. Was he a bit smitten? It was hard to tell.

"I told you on the phone I needed help doing some mixing, but in reality..." I sucked in a deep breath before admitting the truth. "Do you know that I accidentally summoned Satan at Christmas?"

CeCe's teacup froze halfway to her waiting lips. Amusement lit up her eyes. "No?"

"Okay, so, yeah. I tried to summon Santa, and Satan is who came. He likes it here, and he's moved in next door." I pointed in the direction of his house.

"Oh-kay." The saucer tinkled as she set her cup back in it. "That can't be good."

I shrugged. "It's not been *bad* exactly, but Luci comes with a certain amount of, shall I say, *influence*. He can compel people to do as he wants, sort of enchant them."

CeCe whistled through her bottom teeth. "A rare ability."

"Right. So, I found an anti-compulsion spell, but I need juice to make it stick. Owen and I tried, but he's a full necromancer. He can do spells, but he doesn't generally have a lot of power behind them. Not like a witch does. And though I'm half necromancer, I need some help doing this."

CeCe rolled up her sleeves. "Let me at it. What are we charming?"

Jumping to my feet, I walked around the chairs toward the kitchen. "I have all my potion ingredients and stuff in here."

At the back of the kitchen, I opened the doors to the conservatory with a flourish, letting CeCe go in ahead of me. "Ohh," she said. "Black Oleander. That's a rare poison."

I let her admire my plants for a few moments before opening the grimoire to the appropriate charm.

"Are you trying to get rid of me again?" Luci asked, appearing out of the blue at the end of the conservatory, right in front of CeCe. We both jumped and I screamed.

She stepped back with her hand at her throat. "My goodness," she said. "You're the devil."

He tipped an invisible hat as he gave a slight bow. "At your service."

CeCe turned to me with an eyebrow up. "Well, they do say the devil is handsome."

Luci preened as CeCe walked to the table and inspected the objects I had laid out there. I'd gone into town and purchased several necklaces, bracelets, and rings from a local craft shop. "I was hoping we could charm these so I could let my loved ones wear them. I'd rather they not be able to be compelled."

Luci scoffed. "Hey," he said in indignation. "I'm standing right here."

I arched my eyebrow at CeCe but ignored the devil. "Are you up for the charm?" I asked.

CeCe clasped her hands together, then pulled off a pretty diamond ring from her right hand. "Only if I get one, too."

"Deal," I said, and turned the book so she could read it, too. "Now, according to this, we brew a potion and until it comes to a boil, we have to say this incantation over and over. That part will be dull, but once it's boiled, we just dip the objects in the potion, and we're done."

CeCe nodded and squinted down at the ingredient list. "Seems simple enough."

Luci pulled the book toward him. "Yeah, if you

have enough juice. If you're not strong enough, the incantations won't take hold and the potion won't do anything but taste bad." He smacked his lips and grimaced. "Trust me."

"We'll take your word for it." I gave him a dry smile and started gathering ingredients.

"You know," Luci said. "Black jade holds hexes, curses, and charms better than other stones."

I looked at the jewelry. None of it was black jade. "How do I even know you're telling the truth?"

CeCe winced. "He is. I actually knew that."

Pursing my lips, I narrowed my eyes at Luci. "Conjure us a bunch, please."

He mouthed at me for a moment before snapping his teeth together, then waved his hand over the table. A handful of black jade stones appeared beside the jewelry. "I can't believe I'm helping you make sure I can't influence people."

"If you're as charming as they say you are, you don't need compulsion to get people to do as you'd like." CeCe fluttered her eyelashes at the devil. I wasn't sure if she was teasing him or maybe she liked flirting with danger.

Either way. I didn't think he'd hurt her, at least.

When it was time to turn the heat on the potion, we joined hands around the table as Luci poked around in my plants. I tried my best to ignore him as we chanted, but it was difficult. *"Et perspicuitati conducit,"* we repeated over and over.

I focused as hard as I could, but when Luci snapped off a piece of black oleander, then sniffed it, my attention wavered.

Then the fool popped it into his mouth and started chewing. "Luci!" I exclaimed. "That's highly poisonous."

Luci grinned and chewed. "And absolutely delicious."

"Focus," CeCe hissed, then went back to chanting. I joined her.

Thirty minutes later, we had several pieces of jewelry as well as a handful of black jade stones, all covered in anti-compulsion charms. All in all, it had been a successful day, even with Luci looking constantly over our shoulders. And apparently immune to black oleander.

"Well, this was fun," CeCe said. She pocketed one of the jade stones and put on the ring we'd charmed. "I want us to get together again soon, okay? We can play with some powerful spells, see if we can't irritate the devil."

Luci sniffed. "We'll see." He winked. "It was a

pleasure doing business with you, ladies." He tipped his imaginary hat again and disappeared.

Once Luci was gone, I turned to CeCe. "You and Lorelai said you wanted to talk to me about the accidents."

She leaned in and whispered, "Be careful. I don't think they were accidents. Someone is using dark magic."

"Do you have any guesses on who?"

CeCe frowned. "No. It's more intuition. But it's too much of a coincidence that it's only coven members dying." Her phone beeped and after she checked it, she said, "I have to go. We do have to get together again soon."

I walked CeCe out. Stepping out on the porch I saw Luci watering his roses. In the dark. Creepy, nosey neighbor. I waved and went back inside, shaking my head. Whatever was going on, at least Shipton Harbor was never boring.

CHAPTER TWELVE

"So, I have to ask..." I peeked at Drew out of the corner of my eye as my stomach rolled with anxiety. He slowed, approaching the stop sign at the end of my street. Taking a deep breath, I tried to will away the dread burning my insides. "I don't have any right to ask. We haven't said anything to each other about exclusivity or anything like that."

After glancing in the rearview mirror, he turned his head and waited at the stop sign, his features a mask of confusion. "What is it?" His voice was full of concern, not a note of suspicion. "I don't mind you asking me anything."

"I went in to pick up dinner at Guac On! the other night on my way home from the bookstore," I said carefully.

He looked in the mirror again but must've seen no cars coming because he returned his attention to me instead of going. "Yeah?"

"And I saw you there with a woman." I threw up my hands, waving them between us. "Now, we've made no claims on one another, and in fact, I'm not truly wanting to nail this down as something super exclusive or like a—a commitment or something." My words came out rushed and in a bit of a panic. I had no idea what I was saying. I was just a rambling mess.

The corners of Drew's lips tipped up. Great, he thought I was nuts. I tried to explain and pull myself out of this mess. "I just think that if we *are* going to date other people, we should maybe make some ground rules." I sucked in a deep breath. "Like, maybe giving the other person a heads up when we might be dating in town. I'd rather not *actually* run into you on another date if possible."

Especially when it was likely that I'd get jealous and hex his date, which I had no right to do. Or claim him as mine. Did I?

Did I want to?

"Ava," Drew said gently, drawing my attention back to him. "It's not what it looked like."

Oh, I hated that line. That was always the first

thing they said when caught cheating. I couldn't stand the thought that Drew might turn out to be one of *those* guys.

"No, you don't have to make an excuse or anything." I turned straight in my seat and clutched my knees, wishing I had something to do with my hands. "I'm not old-fashioned or anything. This is all fine." Fine. It was *fine*.

"Ava." We both jumped when a horn tooted behind us, a short sound that made me think the driver wasn't mad, just letting us know they were back there. Drew cranked down the window on his old truck and waved out the window. "Sorry!"

He turned onto Main Street toward the town's only bowling alley. "That was my sister."

Sister? Now it made sense. The younger woman. The way she looked at him. It was love for a big brother. I sighed in relief before I could stop myself.

"Oh," I said in a small voice and scooted down in my seat. I desperately wanted to crawl under the seat. Damn it. Why had I let my mouth run away from me? I knew darn well that it could've been his sister or cousin or something. I'd even told myself that repeatedly.

"She was in town but just passing through. We had dinner and she went on her way, traveling south to see her grandkids." He winked at me. "And I *want* to be exclusive. I take it you don't?"

Great. My verbal diarrhea had put me in the middle of it this time. "Well, I do, actually. But I still want to take it super slow." Shoot! Admitting that was scary. I'd rather have faced something undead.

He nodded and covered my hand with his, giving a small squeeze. His touch made me relax a little. "I'm okay with that. I know it's got to be incredibly difficult dating again after losing your husband."

The silence stretched between us. "It is," I said finally. "But a large part of me is ready. A smaller part feels incredibly guilty for moving on at all. He was the great love of my life. Am I allowed to have that *possibly* happen again?"

Heavy talk, mentioning love, but I wanted to be honest with Drew. He was a good man, and these were my true feelings. Plus, there'd definitely been sparks in the kisses we'd shared on a few occasions. Sparks I hadn't felt in five years. I wanted to see if they would catch and cause a wildfire.

He parked at the bowling alley, then turned in his seat. "I'm not sure if you've bowled here before?" His words held sarcasm.

With a laugh, I patted his knee. "Honey, you

forget I grew up here. I remember when they opened this place."

He nodded and sighed. "Well, I hope you don't mind, but they have the best onion rings on the planet in there, and their salads are delicious if you don't want something heavy. I recommend the burger, though, if you don't mind the grease."

"I remember," I whispered. "And I love the grease. Salads are for non-date nights."

We decided to sit in the dining area and load up on calorie-laden yumminess before I kicked his firm behind in bowling.

So much had happened in the few days since we last spoke. More since we'd last *seen* each other, though we texted each other at least once a day. Usually just a brief check-in about the case. But he hadn't checked in with me yesterday, so I hadn't had the chance to tell him what I found out from CeCe, which wasn't a whole of more than we already knew. "Oh, I almost forgot."

I reached into my pocket and pulled out a silver men's ring with a black jade setting that was infused with the anti-compulsion potion CeCe and I cooked up a couple of nights ago.

Drew lifted a brow. "What's that?"

"A gift." I smiled and slid it across the table. "It's

infused with magic. A charm to protect against Luci's compulsion and other evil things."

He picked it up and placed it on the middle finger of his right hand. "Thank you."

A warmth settled inside me. "CeCe helped me with the spell. And it gave us a chance to talk about the *accidents*."

I told him about Yaya's imprint and finding the coin that was on my mother when she died. "The coin is the same as the others: a bird with flames. And her witch's mark was blackened, which means some sort of magical death, most often means murder."

I didn't need to say that my *mother* was murdered out loud. Drew connected the dots quickly and covered my hand. I rolled mine over and held his.

"How was the coven meeting?"

I shrugged, easing my hand from his to pick up an onion ring. "I'd say boring. But it was also interesting. I knew they were snotty before, but they don't get involved with the community at all. It's like they live separate from humans or try to, as much as possible."

I told him about the twins, how odd they seemed and Bevan, how it seemed like he didn't like anyone.

"I didn't sense strong enough emotions from any of them that would warrant them killing their own."

"Yet, it is a witch who is cursing the coins?"

I nodded. "I think so unless there is a powerful demon running around." I snorted as Lucifer popped into my mind. "Besides my new neighbor. But Luci wouldn't let one of his Hell buddies run rogue, would he?"

"I agree with you. I think he enjoys it here too much to let a demon spoil it for him." Drew took a bite of an onion ring and chewed before speaking again. "My hunch is this is a witch with a grudge."

That was my thought too. But we'd talked shop long enough. Wanting to change the subject to something more date-related, I asked, "Where are you from?"

One corner of his mouth dipped, making a sexy half frown. "Asheville, North Carolina. My family has an obscene amount of property in the mountains. They use it for hunter central and HQ. Training and so on."

Something dark passed through his irises.

"You didn't like it there?" I chewed, giving him time to answer but he replied immediately. No hesitation.

"Hated it." He took a drink of his beer. "I never

understood the purpose of killing and torturing beings only because they were different or not human. Especially when those beings were innocent of crimes. Most were just trying to live a normal life and wanted to be left alone."

"So you moved to Shipton Harbor where there is a really old family line of witches?" I was sure the hunters knew of my family bloodline. It went back hundreds of years. At least my mother's side did.

He smiled. "I moved here about ten years ago, joined the police force, and was voted Sheriff two years ago. I like it here. And my family knows not to come here hunting. This is my domain. If they come to visit, they aren't to stay more than a few days."

Wow. That was interesting. I knew he had a good relationship with his mom and, it seemed, his sister. He'd told me he and his dad didn't always see eye to eye. I didn't know he could just tell them not to hunt in the area he lived in and they would actually respect his wishes. "So we can rule out hunters for cursing the witches?"

"At least hunts from my family. But don't worry, I would know the moment another hunter came into the area. No one but Lily has been nearby since my parents visited last summer." He finished off his last onion ring.

"Does your no hunting in Shipton rule extend outside the family?"

"Hunters don't follow a single ruling body. They pretty much govern themselves. That's why it's easy for those like Scarlett to get away with killing senselessly for so long." He watched me for a few moments, which made me a little uncomfortable.

Don't get me wrong, I could've stared at him all day, every day for the rest of my life just as long as he didn't stare back.

Um, did I just say every day for the rest of my life? Well, don't tell Drew. I didn't need him getting pushy and demanding on me.

CHAPTER THIRTEEN

*O*wen and Wallie both were going straight onto my crap-list. I'd given them an entire week's notice to be ready for this party. But, no, they had other, more important things to do besides being by my side like the supportive family they were supposed to be.

I didn't want to be rude and cancel altogether but going by myself had caused my nerves to go haywire on me. Taking a deep breath and releasing it, I tried to exhale all of the frustration that had built up inside me since Miriam died in a yarn cocoon. I had to find out who killed her and Lorelai. Because that killer was most likely—I was a hundred percent sure—the same one who killed my mother and Larry.

What better way to start looking than with the coven? So I had to go to the fancy party.

Alone. Darn them!

Wallie, I understood. It was March, almost spring break, and he had big tests to study for. But Owen could've rescheduled his date.

He'd taken a shine to Kelly, the owner of the bakery beside the bookstore. When he worked shifts for Clint, he liked to stop in and sample Kelly's eclairs. And had plans to sample other things.

I shook out of that thought with a shudder. I was not thinking about what he could possibly be sampling. Kelly was beautiful and one of the nicest people I'd met in a long time. Owen deserved to have a real life and spend it with someone. I just didn't need any visuals that I couldn't unsee.

And they could've rescheduled their date.

I pulled up to the valet, and as I slowed the car, I stared at the entrance of CeCe's house. Well, mansion. Light, new age music drifted from the open door.

A tingle of magic caressed my skin as Luci appeared in my passenger seat in an all-black tux. I jumped and swallowed a scream. After my heart started working again, I glared at him.

Darn him. He looked amazing. Devilish amazing.

"Hello, darling," he said smoothly, a wicked smile spreading across his face. "Fancy a date for the soirée?"

A date? With the devil? Uh, *no*!

A movement behind Lucifer, outside the car, caught my attention. Great. The valet walked forward, one of the coven member's teenage sons again, and waited with his hands crossed while I turned to glare at Luci. "What are you doing here?" I hissed.

"I stay apprised of the local coven's goings-on and imagine my dismay when I learned you had no date to tonight's festivities. I had to come to my new friend's rescue." He winked at me. "Where is the beau anyway?"

Friend? I wasn't sure I'd call us that. Not even close. And as for *beau*... "I'll have you know; he is working. Not that it is any of your business. Besides, I don't need a date," I said, glancing out at the kid. "And this isn't the sort of function I could just bring anyone to."

Could Luci disappear without the guy knowing he'd ever been in the car? I didn't think so. "Shoot," I muttered. "You're going to have to go with me. He's seen you."

Luci's face brightened in a wide grin. "Fantastic." He threw open the passenger door and launched himself out of the car. "I've got her door," he called and hurried around the car. Oh, great.

The boy stepped back, and Luci opened my door with a flourish, our clothing and his behavior so out of place for my Hyundai, Dia.

But then, I didn't fit in at this fancy house, anyway. Mansions weren't exactly my style. If one of my books took off and started making tons of money, I still wouldn't want to buy another home. Not only because my coastal house seemed to have its own personality, but because fancy-schmancy wasn't really in my repertoire.

The dress I'd chosen was long and black, and I had on enough girdles and shapewear under it to keep me from eating or breathing all night. At least it had lace sleeves. They made me feel pretty sexy. Especially in the heels.

But as I started up the stairs to the front door, the heels began to pinch.

Damn. It was going to be a long night.

The door opened on its own and Luci and I

stepped inside. "Wait," I hissed. "Who are we going to say you are?"

He grinned wickedly and waved his hand over his face. He'd done the spell so I could sort of see the glamour and his true face at the same time, though I suspected I was the only one. "Cousin Bertrand, visiting from out of town."

I studied him, and I had to admit it was impressive. To a stranger, no one would think twice if we said we were related. But someone who knew my family would be a little harder to convince. However, Lucifer had transformed into a handsome, older man with grey in his temples and a streak in his bangs that were swept to the side. His skin was a little paler and his jawbone squarer. He'd even changed his eyes green to match mine. Well, not an exact copy. Luci's new eyes were lighter, less dark-magic. I wasn't even sure how he'd pulled that off. The eyes were the portals to our soul. At least that was what I'd always heard.

The click of heels against marble tile brought me out of admiring my new cousin.

I turned and smiled as CeCe walked out of the library. "Ava," she cried. "You came." She hurried out down the hall in a gorgeous crimson gown that hugged her modest curves and flared out about mid-thigh. She looked like a gothic queen with her black hair and pale skin. Bevan Magnus followed her out.

CeCe grabbed my shoulders and pulled me close, pressing a kiss to each cheek. "And who is this handsome fellow?"

"CeCe, this is my cousin. He's from..." Shit. We hadn't said where he was from.

"Florida," Luci said. "I'm Bertrand." He offered CeCe his hand and simpered. "So sorry for the intrusion, but I begged dear cousin Ava to bring me. I adore my coven at home and couldn't wait to meet the people inviting Ava to join their ranks."

"It's no intrusion," CeCe said graciously. "Though I did hope your son and," her voice rose questioningly, "*friend,* Owen, would've been able to come?"

"I'm so sorry, Wallie couldn't get away from his coming tests, and Owen had a prior engagement."

Bevan pushed himself closer. "Pleasure." He held his hand out and looked at Luci with more respect in his eyes than he'd shown me. Of course. "I'm Bevan."

"Bertrand." Luci held out his hand to Magnus. "Call me Bertie."

Now it made more sense. Bevan didn't like

women. Or at least, didn't like women in positions of power. Great.

"Please, come in," Bevan said, holding his hand out. As *Bertie* walked forward, Bevan put his hand at the small of his back.

Maybe it was less about not liking women and more about Bevan liking Bertie. Interesting.

The crowd was small, and CeCe held up her hand. When she started to speak, the room fell silent. "Friends, we're all eager to celebrate the inclusion of Ava in our midst but let us take a moment of quiet for our dear departed witch, Lorelai. A horrible, tragic accident. I propose at the end of our night, we participate in a protection charm together. Our coven has endured an awful coincidence of tragedy lately. Perhaps we can do a bit to turn lady luck around."

The small group clapped quietly.

"To Lorelai," Bevan said, holding his champagne glass up. Someone appeared at my elbow with a tray. I took a glass and raised it.

After a few seconds, Bevan drank, then raised his glass again. "And to Ava, the newest member of our great coven."

Erm, what? I stumbled while leaning toward

CeCe, then quickly righted myself. Bertie-Luci grabbed my elbow for a little added support.

His hand was really warm.

"I'm sorry," I said softly. "But I haven't accepted entry yet, have I?"

CeCe turned to me with wide eyes and a face full of surprise. "We just assumed," she hissed. "We never thought you'd say no after what a wonderful time we all had the other night."

"I mean, it was nice, sure, but I'm not sure I'm the coven type," I said. "I've done things on my own for such a long time."

She stepped back and her face closed down. "Of course. However, you wish to proceed is fine."

Well, shit. I'd offended her. "How about we take it slow?" I asked, feeling like I was talking to Drew again. "And go from there?"

With a sniff, CeCe nodded her head. "That's fine."

She went to leave, but I stopped her with a hand on her arm. "This is sudden. No one mentioned that I'd be inducted tonight. You must understand that the history my family had with the coven isn't puppies and rainbows."

CeCe relaxed and she took my hand in hers. "That was before I took over as coven leader. Your mother's death was a huge hit to all of us. She was loved among all the coven members as were Winnie and Esme."

I hadn't heard anyone say Yaya's first name in a long time. It sent a pulse of sadness through me.

"Did you know your mother was voted coven leader a few weeks before she died?" CeCe swiped a finger under one of her eyes. "We've all lost too many friends and family."

I stilled and studied CeCe. I hadn't known Mom was to be the coven leader. "No, I didn't know that. Then again, after she died, I withdrew from magic. Especially my necromancer powers. Yaya and Winnie pulled away from the coven then."

CeCe nodded. "I stepped in after that. We gave your family the space they needed to grieve. But we had hoped that you would rejoin. I don't tolerate prejudice against others and have opened membership to all magic born."

But they kept the coven to thirteen members. No more, no less. Some traditions didn't go away. And there were only witches. *All* didn't mean the same thing to both of us.

At the sound of her name, CeCe glanced up to see Bevan calling her. She sighed. Before she let go of my hand, she sent a thought to me. *"The High Witch position is yours as it was your mother's. Just say the word, and I'll step down and pass on the torch. Ah, it's a potion, actually."*

While I processed her words, she drew me into a hug and said out loud, "Welcome to the coven, Ava." A potion? Why a potion?

Then she darted off to tend to Bevan. I watched her leave, stunned. Why did she tell me that telepathically? Was it not public knowledge? Then again, she believed there was a killer inside the coven and maybe didn't want him or her knowing I was next in line to lead the coven.

How in the Hell did she send me her thoughts? That was a trick I needed to learn. I wonder if Yaya's imprint knew how.

I caught Bevan's stare... more like glare. For a brief moment, his aura shifted to a darker grey, then was back to its usual blue. Interesting.

A laugh drew my attention to the other side of the room where Luci...er *Bertie* was entertaining a couple of female witches. Lenna and Mai, I believed were their names.

Frowning, I made a mental note to make more charms for the coven. When I stepped forward, one of the twins appeared in front of me. I jumped and moved back a few steps.

He didn't materialize or anything. I just hadn't seen him approach. Damn it. I needed to pay attention.

"Welcome to the coven."

I forced a smile. "Thank you."

He stared at me, so I stared back, lifting both brows because I wasn't talented enough to do the one brow lift. Dark magic flowed from him, tingling my skin. It surrounded me, teasing my dark powers. I didn't like it. But I couldn't run out the door because that would make me look weak. A weak prey was dead prey.

"Can I help you with something?" I asked, amping up my dark magic.

One side of his mouth lifted in a smirk. "Do be careful. Coven members haven't had much good luck lately."

Once again, I was left standing in the center of the room with my mouth open in shock as I watched him walk out.

This was going to be a long night.

After the twin, whom I never got to ask which one he was, the evening was pleasant. My guess the twin was Brandon because he was the creepier of the two. But I could have been wrong.

The other coven members were nice, and I didn't

get bad vibes from anyone else besides the twins and Bevan.

Luci came up to me a while later, after I'd talked to everyone at least once. Some twice. "You look ready to go."

"I am. These shoes are killing me. I've had enough playing nicey-nice to the witches." I laughed at my joke and quickly realized that I was starting to like some of these witches.

Well, that was a twist I hadn't seen coming.

Luci took my arm and curled it in his. "Come, Ava, dear, Let's go home."

"Thank you. You know, for crashing the party and pretending to be my cousin."

"Any time, dear." Luci really came through tonight and almost seemed normal.

I had to remember. No matter how nice he was, I was still finding out a way to send him back to Hell.

CHAPTER FOURTEEN

My sofa had never been so comfortable. After drinking entirely too much champagne last night and letting Luci drive me home, I didn't want to be anywhere but right here, watching bad reality TV bundled up in my fluffiest robe.

Just a lazy, relaxing day.

So—of course!—my doorbell rang.

Great. I hoped it wasn't anything that would involve me leaving the house.

"I got it," Larry called from the kitchen. Or preferably the couch.

"Don't answer it if it's someone that will freak out," I replied, frowning.

He stopped in the living room doorway. "Give me a little credit, Ava."

I would not. The darn skeleton kept forgetting he was all bones. He liked to hang out with the flesh-wearing people too often. I even caught him meditating in the middle of the backyard the other day. It was a good thing my only neighbor close enough to see him was a demon. *The* demon.

"Hello, Officer," Larry said. I sat bolt upright. Please tell me this was not Drew.

"Uh, hello?" Drew replied.

Crap!

Waving my hand over my face, I glamoured myself just enough to not look quite so crazy. Or homeless. I hadn't taken my makeup off before collapsing in bed the night before, so I removed my dark circles and tamed my hair. I didn't mind Drew seeing me without makeup or in my robe, but he didn't need to see the blotchy leftover foundation or my raccoon eyes.

Too bad I couldn't get rid of this hangover so easily. There was a potion cure for a hangover, but it was so disgusting I wouldn't use it. Drinking raw eggs and frog toes wasn't on my list of things to do the day after too much champagne.

"Hello," I said softly as I muted the TV and

scooted over on the couch to make room for Drew to sit next to me.

"Hey, there," he said, studying me for a long few seconds. Did he know I was glamouring myself? Probably, since he was a born hunter and was sensitive to magic. "Late night?" He looked at his watch and raised his eyebrows.

I moaned and let my head hang back. "Yeah. There was a coven meeting. The invitation said fancy dress, and when I got there, it turned out it was a party to celebrate me accepting their invitation."

Drew furrowed his brow. "But at our date last weekend, you said you weren't sure if you'd join. I got the impression you were leaning toward not."

I snorted. "They couldn't conceive of the possibility that I might refuse them."

He nodded. "I see."

"That's not the best part. Although, this ended up being a big help to me. As I pulled up to the party, Lucifer appeared in the car beside me."

Drew's jaw dropped. "What happened?"

I sucked in a deep breath and thought about how Luci had captivated the coven. "I don't know, having him there took the heat off of me a bit. He was charming and made the rounds, so I wasn't the only new person in the room. He introduced himself as my distant cousin, in for a visit." I imitated his British accent when I spoke the last sentence.

With a chuckle, Drew shook his head. "Didn't they recognize him? He was at the Christmas party, and I imagine several of the covens came to that. And he's not exactly been hiding from the town. He goes out and about often."

"No, he glamoured his appearance so he looked different." I shrugged. "I'm not saying I want him to stick around, but it was nice having him on my side last night. I was able to observe everyone better."

Drew pursed his lips. "Well, at least he did something nice."

"Hey," I said. "Paris was nice."

We both dissolved into laughter. However nice it was, it had also been freaky and had given Drew some insane motion sickness. "What brings you here this morning?" I asked.

"Well," he said and pulled a folded piece of paper out of his jacket pocket. "I've been doing some research."

The white paper crinkled as he unfolded it and handed it to me. "I've been searching all cases of accidental deaths in the county, looking for patterns, and there's a big one."

"Oh?" I asked as I took the paper from him. He explained the names and dates listed on the paper.

"Yeah. These are all people that died with an odd coin in their pockets. Most of the coins were given back to families, but in one case, there was no next of kin. The body was cremated, and the ashes were buried cheaply in the town cemetery. I have the coin here." He pulled a small baggie from his pocket and handed it over.

Sure enough, it looked exactly like the ones we'd found so far. "No," I breathed.

"Yes, and get this. That death was in the seventies." He stared at me with his eyebrows up and nostrils flared.

"You guys keep records and personal effects that long?" I asked.

He nodded. "Forever, really. If we run out of room, we'll rent a storage place or build a shed, but you never know what might come up that you need evidence like this for." He pointed to the paper. "Case in point."

Reaching over, Drew took the paper and shuffled it. I hadn't even realized there was a second page. "This is a list of all deaths that weren't attributed to natural causes in the county going back to the sixties, no matter if coins were noted or not. Accidents and murders."

I browsed the list. Most of them were car wrecks. But there were more that were freakish, out of the norm like the umbrella thing or a freak lightning storm. Some of the others included smothered by a pile of winter coats, drowned in a vat of molasses, slipped on an orange peel and broke neck, a firework blew up in one person's face.

"Holy crap," I whispered. "This is terrible." So many people and they all had a coin found on them.

I lifted the bag with the coin up. "Can I take this out? The coin my Yaya found on Mom still had a little of the curse left over. I want to put it in salt-water just to be sure."

He stared at the coin and nodded. "Yeah, do that."

Setting the papers on the coffee table I stood and waved Drew to follow. "Step into my magical office."

He chuckled, but I caught a spark of concern light up his teal eyes for a second. It occurred to me at that moment that he wasn't used to magic and all the craziness that had happened over the last several months.

I turned to face him, and he stopped short, his hands resting on my hips. My breath caught as heat filled every part of me. "You don't have to come into the conservatory if it makes you uncomfortable."

He lifted one hand and ran his knuckles down my cheek. A soft sigh slipped from my lips as I leaned into his touch. It'd been too long since I gave myself over to a man. Clay had been my only lover.

"Magic is a big part of you. Dark, light, and everything in between." He slid his hand around to cup the back of my head. Then his lips pressed against mine and my world exploded in a rush of power and desire.

He ended the kiss and rested his forehead on mine. "I want all of you, Ava. You never have to hide who you are from me."

Something bloomed in my heart. For most of my life, I hid what I was, my power. I did it with Clay to keep the peace with his family. Recently, I caught myself doing it with Drew because he was a born hunter. Even though he swore he denied that half of him.

I placed my hand over his heart. "You don't have to hide who you are either." I press a finger from my other hand to his lips. "Hunters are born with magic and other abilities. I've done some research. You don't have to hunt down innocent paras just because you're a hunter. Use your gifts for good."

A seductive smile formed on his handsome face. "I will if you will."

"Deal!" I linked my fingers with his and pulled him toward the kitchen. That was when I noticed Alfred standing in the archway to the kitchen, watching us.

Maybe I was crazy, but I sensed emotions coming from him. Concern and protectiveness were the strongest, but there was also caution and dislike. Did Alfred not like Drew?

I stopped in front of him and his gaze softened as he looked at me. Then he handed his tablet to me. On the screen he'd typed, **"What would you like for lunch? Dinner?"**

"You don't have to cook all the time. We can order out. Or Drew and I..." I turned to Drew, noticing for the first that he was dressed in plain clothes. A pair of dark blue jeans and a charcoal grey t-shirt. "I guess you aren't working today. Did you have other plans?"

"I was going to ask you the same thing."

"Looks like we're spending the day together." I tugged him through the kitchen to the conservatory. I heard Alfred grunt as he took steaks out of the freezer, making an executive decision about dinner. That was fine with me. I wasn't picky.

I went straight to the sink and filled a glass bowl with water while pulling out the salt from the shelf over it. From the corner of my eye, I watched Drew drift over to the plants lined up on shelves along the far wall. "Don't touch the ones on the top shelf. They're poison."

He looked at me with a raised brow. "Should I ask why you have poisonous plants?"

I shrugged. "You never know when you need them." Then I started laughing. "They were Aunt Winnie's and for some reason lived through the last year without anyone tending to them. So I take it as a sign that they need to stay where they are."

I sure hoped I'd never have to use them in a spell or on anyone. Killing people by poison was not on my to-do list. Ever. But there were still some nonlethal spells that required them. Until I learned how to use them properly, they would stay on that shelf like little creepers, watching over the others.

Once the saltwater was ready, I took the coin out of the bag and dropped it in the water. The same grey smoke puffed out of the water as soon as the coin went under.

"Was that...?"

"The curse, yes. What was left of it." I faced him, and he moved closer. His clean cedar scent enveloped me, making me want things I hadn't had in *so* long.

"What did you want to do today?"

A few naughty thoughts flashed in my mind. But I said, "I'm open to whatever."

Desire flashed in his gaze, making my flesh hot. "There is the Founders' Party going on downtown."

"That sounds great." It was the perfect thing I needed to keep my mind off the accidents-slash-murders and the fact that I hadn't a clue who was doing it. "I just need to clean up and change."

Clint had wrangled Owen into helping with it, to my delight and his disgruntlement.

I took the coin out of the water, dried it off, and placed it back into the bag. Drew stuffed it back into his pocket. "I'll need to return it to evidence."

Rushing upstairs and to my room, I heard water running in the upstairs bathroom. When I passed it, I stopped and stared with my mouth open, truly shocked. After the things I'd seen over the last few months, I hadn't expected to be shocked again. Ever.

Larry stood in front of the sink, water running, and a washcloth in his hand. And he was cleaning out his eye sockets.

Eww. It was disturbing, yet I couldn't look away. How the hell could he see to know he was cleaning them thoroughly?

Owen stopped next to me. "That is not right."

"Tell me about it." We stared in silence as he finished with his eye sockets and wiped down all of his... uh, *face*, and even his teeth.

Just then Larry turned to us and we jumped. "Morning...well afternoon, guys." Then he turned off the water, draped the washcloth over the faucet, and then left the bathroom, walking past us like it was completely normal for a skeleton to clean his eyes sockets.

When did my life take a turn to Crazytown?

CHAPTER FIFTEEN

"*I*'m more excited than I thought I'd be." I had butterflies in my stomach, but I was thrilled to be doing something other than reading grimoires and raising the dead.

We walked down the sidewalk from the spot we'd had to park in. It was a good thing my date was the town sheriff, otherwise, we'd have been just as likely to find a parking spot in my yard, way outside of town.

Everyone in the county had turned up for this shindig. I hadn't remembered it being this busy when I was a kid.

"You know," Drew said as his knuckles brushed mine, sending a jolt of pleasure through me. "Your family were founders."

I glanced at him out of the corner of my eye as we stepped onto the sidewalk lining Main Street, leaving his SUV in the police department parking lot. "I do know that. How do you?"

He shrugged. "I read the founders' book." For some reason, he didn't quite meet my eyes.

Tipping my voice up into an innocent lilt, I gave him a megawatt smile. "You did?" I asked. "Whatever for?"

He snickered. "Don't act like that. I can't be interested in what's going on in my town?"

We crossed the street at the town's only stoplight, heading for the big gazebo in the park in the middle of town. All of the shops were designed in a square around it with the police station and fire station just down the road.

"Hey!" Carrie called. She had a bean bag toss game set up. "Play? Proceeds go toward getting new desks in the Kindergarten classrooms."

"Sure," Drew said, pulling out his wallet. "How much?"

"A dollar gets you three throws. If you win, you get to pick a prize from the prize bucket."

I peered into the bucket and clasped my hands together. "Please, win me a prize," I said. "I *need* this tiara." There was a silver, plastic tiara in the bucket that would look amazing on me.

Drew grinned and tossed the little bean bag in the air a few times before turning to the table.

"Stand there." Carrie pointed to a piece of tape on the grass. "The blue tape is for adults. Green is for kids. Pink is for toddlers."

"Whoops," Drew said. He was standing on the green and backed up. "Here we go. A tiara for my lady."

I clapped as he threw and missed completely. "Aw, that's okay." I tried to give him a supportive and encouraging look, but it mostly came across as me just laughing at him.

"Uh-huh," he said. "I'm just getting warmed up."

He threw again and tipped the top bottle on the triangle. "See?" he said. "Third time's a charm."

"Right." I squinted at the last beanbag in his hand. As he threw it, and while it sailed through the air, I twitched my finger and set it on more of a straight and true course.

Unfortunately, Drew had thrown it very wide, so when I corrected it, there was a noticeable curve. As the bottles clattered to the ground, both Drew and Carrie eyed me suspiciously.

I looked around the square, pretending they

weren't staring at me and trying to figure out if I'd helped him. With a small jump, I faked noticing they were staring at me. "What? Oh! You won! Yay!" I hurried forward and grabbed the cheap tiara from the prize bucket. "Awesome."

Drew took it and carefully positioned it on my head, shaking his own as he did. "Cheater," he said quietly.

"I don't know what you're talking about, but I want to go over there next." I pointed toward the next booth. "I think we're expected there."

"What do you mean?" Drew eyed the dunking booth suspiciously. "Why would we be expected?"

Luci walked around the large booth and clapped when he saw us. "Oh, lovely. Our first volunteer. Come around here and get changed, please."

Drew turned to me with wide, panicked eyes. "What is happening?"

"Well," I said carefully. "Luci here asked me yesterday if you'd be game to take a turn in the dunking booth, and I said sure, why not?"

His face went from shocked to scrunched up and suspicious. "Are you trying to get me to get you back?"

I shrugged. "Perhaps. Maybe I find it interesting

to see what you think you can come up with to pay me back."

He laughed low in his throat. Not quite amusement, more of a promise of retribution. "Oh, I look forward to coming up with something."

"Come along," Luci called. "I've got a little changing tent back here."

Drew walked around the tank but kept his narrowed gaze on me, his eyes promising I was going to regret this.

Whatever he came up with would be totally worth it.

Two minutes later, he climbed into the tank and sat on the little pedestal in a pair of swim trunks. He shivered and crossed his arms around his wide chest.

He had a dusting of hair on his chest, not much, but what I could see of it was just beginning to go gray. Like the hair at his temples.

His stomach hadn't begun to paunch, even though he was certainly old enough for it. Instead, he sat there, shivering, with the body of an older man who took care of himself. Thick, firm muscles. Broad shoulders.

Oh, geez. Now I was nervous about the fact that we might, in the near future, see one another totally naked. Utterly in the buff. My insecurities about my body flashed through my mind, but I shoved them to the side as I fished five dollars out of my purse.

"Come one and come all!" Luci said in a booming voice. "Dunk the sheriff for a mere five dollars! All proceeds go to helping the firehouse get new hoses!"

I chuckled and Luci gave me a dirty look. Not many of us even knew he was the actual devil, but at least a handful of townspeople would likely get a snicker out of the fact that the devil was raising money to help put out fires. Irony.

"I'll go!" I called. Unbeknownst to either Luci or Drew, I sent a small spell to the water. Drew was cold now, and he'd be cold when he emerged from the water, but I made sure the water would be warm and comfortable. He'd want to get dunked to warm up. It was the least I could do after voluntelling him that he was dunking.

Luci took my money and handed me three balls. Stepping back to the line in the grass, I squinted at the bullseye and pulled my arm back.

"No cheating!" Drew called.

"How could she cheat?" Clint asked from behind me. "She either hits it or she doesn't."

I turned and winked at my part-time boss. Owen

and I had managed to keep our supernatural side from him thus far. Hopefully, it stayed that way.

"You ready to get wet?" I asked Drew.

He rolled his eyes. "Sure."

"What you probably don't know about me was that I played softball all through high school and could've had a partial scholarship to college playing softball."

I didn't need magic to do this. Poor Drew. His face darkened as he glared at me.

Aiming carefully, I put just enough spin on the ball and let it fly.

Straight into the bullseye. And not even a drop of magic.

Drew yelped and his arms flew up as the podium fell, and he slipped off and into the water. Hey, it could've been a lot worse. I could've left the water cold.

A small crowd had gathered, including Olivia and Sam. They cheered the hardest as Drew climbed back onto the seat again. "Okay," he called. "You got me. Let someone else go."

He wiped the water from his eyes as I held out the next ball. Olivia darted forward. "I believe I will!" she chirped.

As I handed her the ball, I winked at Drew.

"Don't worry!" I called. "She wasn't on the school softball team!"

"That's right!" Olivia agreed. "I played on my *church* softball team." She flung the ball at the bullseye and nailed it, sending Drew splashing back into the water.

He came up sputtering. "Okay, the next person isn't allowed to have been on any softball team."

When he climbed up and looked back out at us, it was just in time for me to hand the last ball I'd paid for to Sam.

Drew's face pinched as he glared. "Deputy, kindly remember I'm your boss."

Sam's face split into a broad grin. "I know. And you're off duty." He pulled his arm back, then addressed Drew again. "Have we ever talked about my favorite weekend pastime in college?"

Drew shook his head slowly.

"Darts." Sam threw the ball and rocked on his heels as it hit its target. "Not quite the same as being good at softball, but it gets the job done," he said as Drew splashed around in the tank.

After another round of dunking Drew, we let the kids that had lined up to sink the sheriff have their turn.

Drew was relieved. I knew my payback was

going to be wicked by the playful glares he sent me. It would be all worth it.

Hell, it was already worth it to see him without his shirt.

Half an hour later, one of the firefighters replaced Drew in the dunk tank. Once he was in dry clothes, I used magic to dry his hair. He was all smiles and admitted he had fun. But still said he would get me back.

By the end of the day, we were walking hand in hand. I didn't realize it when it happened, but I liked it. I liked him. One thing I learned about Drew was underneath that alpha male, sheriff façade, he knew how to have fun. And he was so easy to talk to.

I looked forward to more dates with him.

CHAPTER SIXTEEN

"*U*no!" Sammie yelled, doing a little dance in his chair. "I beat you again!"

Alfred grunted and threw his cards down on the table, then he wagged his finger at Sammie while the child giggled mercilessly. "You can never beat me, Alfie!" he crowed.

"Don't be a sore winner," Olivia called.

I chuckled as I walked back toward the living room with mugs of tea. The ghoul, the skeleton, and the kid had set up a card game in the dining room, within eyesight of us in the living room.

She'd come over since I didn't have a shift at the bookstore, and I'd just finished writing the first draft of my latest manuscript. I liked to give my books a week to breathe before going back in and starting my second run-through.

We'd been going through the occult books that had finally come in at Clint's shop, looking for a way to *un*summon the devil.

There were shockingly few spells to undo a summons, and the only ones we'd found had failed. The devil was not an average, garden-variety demon. Just our luck.

No, he was a fallen angel tasked with the job of ruling Hell. And there was nothing about vanquishing an angel.

Olivia's phone rang as she sighed and leaned back, rubbing her eyes. "Hey, honey," she chirped when she picked up. Must've been Sam.

Her face fell as she listened. "Oh, no. I'm sorry to hear that." She listened for a few more seconds. "Yes, we'll be right there."

"What is it?" I asked as soon as she hung up.

"We've got another accidental death. Drew wants us to come down and see if we can see anything or sense anything that he can't. They found a coin."

I heaved a big sigh. "Leave Sammie here?" I asked as I jumped up and headed for the foyer and my sneakers. "Owen is here."

"That would be great." She grabbed her jacket. "Owen, Sammie," she called up the stairs.

Sammie came out of the kitchen as Owen stuck his head into the stairwell. "Yes?"

"We've got to run an errand. Alfred is entertaining Sammie, but could you keep an eye on them?"

He nodded. "Sure, no problem. I was about to come down for some lunch, anyway. Has he eaten?"

They arranged for Owen to make a round of PBJs, and we hit the road.

"Have you warned Sammie about Alfred?" I asked. "I mean, he's great with him, but he's still a ghoul."

She nodded as we got into my car. "I did. I told him to keep at arm's reach and always be aware that Alfred is undead. Can't be too careful. I'm glad Owen is there with them."

I'd done a spell on the house a few weeks before. Olivia and I had found it in one of the old grimoires. No harm could come to the innocent in that house now. Nobody could hurt Sammie, though I didn't know if it applied to stuff like accidents or if the little guy fooled around and hurt himself somehow. Still, we both had peace of mind leaving him like this.

"Did Sam say what happened?" I asked. "Or where we're going?"

She gave me a dark look as I pulled to the end of my driveway, waiting on a direction and wondering whether I should go to the left or right. "It's the leader of the coven," she said. "CeCe."

"No." I gasped. "How?"

She knew CeCe from living in town all her life. Also, I'd told her all about both coven meetings and when CeCe came over to help with the charms. "He didn't say. But if they found a coin, I'd be willing to bet it's something weird."

That much was true. My chest tightened at the thought of CeCe dying. I was starting to like her. Then another thought hit me. With CeCe dead, I was next in line to lead the coven. Crap.

"So, to the mansion?" I asked.

"Yep." She sighed. "He did say it's not pretty, so brace yourself."

Ugh. I knew what that meant. It was probably bloody or particularly gory. Not what I wanted to see after just having been there the weekend before.

Sam and Drew met us outside. "Our guys have been over the scene already," Sam said.

Drew put his arm around me, and I sank into him, loving his warmth. "We're officially calling this a string of murders," he said. "The coins are too much coincidence."

"Okay, so you just want me to confirm her witch's mark?" I asked. "I already know she's a witch."

Sam and Drew exchanged a glance. Drew cleared his throat. "Er, actually, I can see the marks. We thought you could try to get her to talk like you tried before. See if she saw anything or knows anything."

"Sure," I said. "I can try. Are we alone here?"

Drew nodded and pulled me closer to him. "Her husband is human, right?"

"I have no idea. She never introduced me to a husband, and the coven members and some of their children were only people here when I was."

Drew sighed. "Okay. The husband is probably human if he wasn't at the coven meetings. We sent him to the station to fill out paperwork. And their children live out of state. They're flying in. We're alone here for the moment."

They led Olivia and me into the house that had magically welcomed me in just a few days before.

CeCe laid in a pool of blood in the doorway of the big entrance hall and her enormous dining room. "What happened?" I asked, moving closer.

Sam said, "She fell."

I peered at the body. "Is that...?" I wasn't sure if what I was seeing was really what I was seeing. "A casserole?"

"Yes," Sam said. "She was on her way into the dining room with a casserole for her and her husband. She tripped and the glass broke, cutting her carotid."

"It's not the blood loss that often kills the person when they cut the carotid," Olivia chirped.

We all turned to stare at her. "What?" she sniffed and tossed her hair back. "I know stuff."

"Well, what is it then?" Drew asked.

"Blood pressure loss to the brain. Eventually, blood loss would do it, sure, but the loss of blood to the brain is the main culprit."

I wasn't sure she was right about that. I'd done a bit of research myself, being an author. I was pretty sure I'd read that a fully cut carotid would cause death by blood loss in five minutes or so.

Not that I was about to contradict Olivia. At least not at the moment. Besides, It didn't matter to me how CeCe died. I was just sorry she was gone.

I knelt beside CeCe and tried to ignore the casserole. Focusing on my would-should have been friend, I called to my magic. "CeCe, who did this to you?"

Her eyes flashed open and my heart dropped to my feet. I would never get used to that. At least CeCe hadn't put a spell on herself so I couldn't raise her. I was about to ask my question again when she started to speak. "Coin is cursed. Don't let him put the coin in your pocket."

"Who?"

"Don't take the coin. He isn't sane." Then her eyes closed, and my magic broke off suddenly.

I pushed magic into her only to have it snap back at me like a rubber band, hitting me in the chest and knocking me on my ass. A groan escaped me as something wet seeped through my jeans. Nice. All I needed was to sit in CeCe's blood.

Drew was at my side in an instant, helping me up. "Thanks," I said resisting the urge to wipe at my blood-soaked ass. "You don't happen to have a change of pants or shorts?"

I was joking but Drew nodded and led me out to his patrol car. Opening the trunk, he pulled out a pair of sweats and handed them to me. "They're clean. I didn't make it to the gym today."

He worked out? Olivia was slipping. She was supposed to tell me all the scoop on everyone in town whether I asked for it or not. That included Drew. Yet, she hadn't told me he had a gym membership. I was going to have to tell her about her failures as the town's busy-body.

Now I'd have to check to see which of the two town gyms he used. You know, so I could get a membership and watch him work out.

"Thank you." I waved a hand and said the incantation for the invisibility spell, then changed out of my soiled jeans and panties. Drew started and turned in a circle. "Ava?"

I giggled and pulled up the pants. Drew's sweats were huge on me and rested on my hips even with the drawstrings tied as tight as they'd go.

Once I released the spell, Drew blinked and frowned. "Where did you go?"

"I was here. I did a spell to take the attention away from me while I changed. It's like being invisible." I moved to Olivia's 4-Runner.

She was waiting for me, looking a little paler than I've ever seen her. Handing me a plastic grocery bag, she said, "You okay? How did your power bounce back like that?"

"I'm not sure. I guess that she was ready to move on. Or it could have been the curse from keeping her from giving a necromancer too much information." I was betting on the latter. "And nothing she said helped us get any closer to figuring out who did this.

Fatigue started to set in, and I yawned. Drew massaged my neck, and I almost told him he'd have to follow me home and give me a full body massage. But I needed sleep.

I turned to him. "Olivia and I are looking through the occult books that I ordered through the bookstore tomorrow. I'll also look through some of the grimoires and see what I can find on this curse."

There had to be a way to track the magic back to the witch who cast it.

Drew kissed my forehead. "I'll call if I find out anything new."

I nodded and climbed into Olivia's SUV and fastened my seat belt.

When we got home, Olivia collected a sleeping Sammie and left with promises of coming back. Or were those threats? I still wasn't sure.

After my new BFF and the cutest kid on earth— besides Wallie of course—left, I went straight to my bedroom and showered. When I exited my bathroom, thankfully wearing my robe, I jumped seeing Alfred sitting on my bed. "Alfie, is something wrong?"

He shook his head and stood, then motioned to the teacup on the nightstand. I walked over and picked up the cup and inhaled. Chamomile and mint. It was what I needed to relax. "Thank you."

I stared at him for a few seconds before reaching out to touch the string hanging from his mouth. He knocked my hand away while shaking his head and moving to the door. "Alfred, I know you can talk. Why don't you want me to take the string out?"

The ghoul was weird about the string. He didn't want it removed. He lifted the tablet I hadn't noticed until then and typed. When he turned it around to show me, the words didn't make sense.

Too soon. Not the right time.

Then Alfred disappeared out of my room.

Why in the world was everyone being so cryptic today?

CHAPTER SEVENTEEN

*B*right and early the next morning...Okay it was 9:00 a.m. but that was still too early for me. Olivia came over with warm, fresh donuts and caramel mocha lattes. The woman was spoiling me with her early morning delivery service.

Sammie was with his grandparents, so we were on our own for the afternoon. The possibilities were endless.

Yet, instead of actual fun, we were hunting for clues and trying, *again*, to trace the magic behind the curse on the coins. Drew was able to steal the coin found on CeCe and had dropped it by the house last night. I'd been asleep so Alfred answered the door. I hoped he didn't answer the door that often. Eventually, we were going to scare a human to death.

When I came downstairs minutes ago, Alfred pointed to the coin on the table. The one Olivia was staring at like it was going to jump up and choke her. Stranger things had happened recently.

"Is that...?"

I nodded. "Yep. The coin they found on CeCe. There is enough of the curse still in the silver that I may be able to trace it this time. So don't touch it."

"Hadn't planned on it. But wouldn't having it in the house, this close to us kill us?" She stared at me with wide eyes.

"No." At least I didn't think so. But, just in case, I had called in backup.

Right on cue, Owen entered the dining room. He eyed the coin suspiciously as he moved to the coffee pot.

Olivia picked up the latte she got for him and handed it to him. "Kelly made this for you."

At the mention of Kelly, the sweet baker and owner of Peachy Sweets, Owen's cheeks colored. He took the cup from Olivia, gave a short shy nod, and took the seat across from me. "The curse is still in there. Not strong, but I can feel it."

"Yeah, I was hoping that we can trace the magical signature of who created the curse." Using my magic, I called to the glass bowl in the conservatory and filled it with water, then directed it to float into the dining room. The salt followed it. Both settled on the center of the table.

Owen sipped his latte and pointed at me. "You know that telekinesis is a rare power for witches."

I stared at him for a moment and said, "So is having three necromancers in the same town."

Olivia perked up. "Three?"

"There were three before William was killed." I dumped salt into the water and twirled my finger over the bowl. The water swirled on its own, mixing the salt.

"Why is it rare? I thought they would network like witches do with their covens." Olivia looked from me to Owen, waiting for an explanation.

Owen answered her because I didn't actually know why. "Necromancers don't work well with others, generally. Ava's not like any other necromancers I've met. Anyway, it's a bad omen to have too many necromancers in one area."

"What kind of bad omen?" I asked while stopping the water in the bowl from swirling.

He shrugged. "I think it's myths passed down. It might have been started by witches not wanting groups of necromancers hanging around. Our powers are dark and go against the natural order, according to witches."

"Like the dead should remain dead," Olivia added. Owen and I nodded.

Owen continued. "There are different stories that tell why. One is that witches cursed necromancers. Others say that it's the combined power of too many in one area. But all the stories say that chaos follows the dark ones. The more there are in one place, the stronger the chaos." Well, that did fit my life lately.

"Wow." Olivia cradled her latte in his hands. "How many are too many?"

I lifted my brows at Owen. I also wanted to know this.

"More than three." Owen picked up a donut from the box.

Note to self—get the coven to check the town for more necromancers.

Speaking of the coven... "CeCe told me that I was next in line to be the high witch."

Owen and Olivia stilled and stared at me for a few seconds. Then Olivia smiled. "That's great. You are the new leader. I mean it's sad that CeCe died, but you're the boss now."

I didn't want to be the boss. Ever. "I have no clue

how to run a coven. And I don't want to talk about it right now." I pointed to the coin and wished I hadn't mentioned it. "We need to do the trace before the curse weakens more."

My theory on the cursed coin was that each one was spelled for a certain person and once the deed was done, the curse faded.

Owen nodded and shoved the donut in his mouth, then wiped his hands with a napkin. After he chewed and swallowed, he held his hands out to me, over the coin. I took them and opened up my magic.

We chanted the simple tracing spell, and the coin began to rattle against the table. Larry came sliding into the room and stopped a few feet from the table. Did he feel our power or the curse from the coin? I didn't have time to ask.

A cloud of smoke rose from the coin and a blurred image formed. But before it cleared, the cloud exploded. Running on instinct, I threw up a bubble around the table at the same time, containing the curse inside it.

"Crap. That backfired." I checked on Olivia. "You okay?"

Her wide eyes met mine. "Yeah. That was...unexpected."

"Definitely," Owen agreed.

LIA DAVIS & L.A. BORUFF

Larry moved forward. "You need to neutralize it before it escapes that bubble."

Great. I didn't need more complications. I definitely didn't need to be cursed to die by a freak accident. Taking a deep breath, I focused on the bowl of salt water. Using my telekinesis—as Owen called it—I pushed the bowl over, spilling the contents on the table and the coin.

The curse dissipated with a hiss. Of course, the donuts and coffees were ruined. "Sorry about breakfast."

Olivia shrugged. "But what happened? The tracer was working then it exploded."

"I think there was an anti-tracker spell mixed in with the curse. Whoever did this is covering his or her butt." I wanted to scream in frustration.

Please, Universe give me a sign. Anything to point me in the right direction to stop the evil witch.

Just then the doorbell rang, sounding like a scream. Olivia and I both jumped. Olivia asked, "What the Hades is that?"

"Doorbell, I think. Winston thinks he's funny." It wasn't the first time the house had slipped in a random doorbell sound.

I stood up and moved toward the door, motioning for Larry and Alfred to hide. With everything that had been happening, I was leery about answering the door at all. Every time I opened it, something else crazy happened. And I had just asked the Universe for a sign. So I was betting on the weird.

I couldn't have been more right.

I opened the door to find Rick and Dana Johnson, the ferret shifter parents. "Hello," I said in shock. "What—are you doing here?" I didn't say it unkindly, but I couldn't imagine why they were back. "How did you find my home?" I stepped back, giving them room to come in.

"Everyone knows where your home is," Dana said. "All the local supernatural folk are plenty familiar with the old white house on the cliffs by the ocean."

I gaped at her as they walked in. "Oh," I whispered. I'd known that most of the Shipton Harbor residents knew the house, but these people lived a few towns over. "What's going on?"

"Our other son wasn't in his bed this morning," Rick said. "And the rest of the pack is getting scared. After we got Ricky's body back, they all started withdrawing, staying home a lot and keeping to themselves."

"Not that we blame them," Dana added. "But

now Ricky's brother, Zane, is missing. We have to find him."

"Come in," I said, gesturing toward the living room. "How long do you think he's been gone?"

They moved into the living room. Owen sat beside Olivia on the sofa, giving our guests the chairs to sit in. I joined my friends.

"I go to bed late," Rick said. "And I always check on him before I lay down. He was there around three."

"And I get up early," Dana continued. "But I didn't check on him, then when he didn't come down for school, I went up. Around seven-thirty. And he was gone. We've contacted anyone in our pack that could help, and only the alpha stepped up. He's tracking Zane with his nose, being a wolf shifter. But we thought maybe you could do a spell or something?"

I met Owen's gaze and he shrugged. "We could certainly try. Did you bring something that belongs to your son?"

Dana nodded and pulled a jacket out of her bag. "He left without a coat." Tears filled her eyes. As I took the cloth from her and opened it up, I realized how small it was. "Wait a minute, how old is Zane?"

"Six," she said softly.

Olivia gasped. "Oh, honey. Did you call the police?"

Rick shook his head. "No. This wasn't a human. No human could sneak into a shifter's home, even a shifter such as us, ferrets."

"This was the same people that took Ricky." Dana sobbed quietly into a handkerchief. "There's no way it's anyone else."

I stood. "Okay," I said. "Let's do this."

CHAPTER EIGHTEEN

We put little Zane's coat on the middle of the coffee table. "Locator spells are simpler than anyone thinks," I said. "It's just a matter of putting magic into an object that belongs to the person." I'd known how to do a locator spell since I was a kid and used to mess with Sam by appearing at all sorts of places when he hadn't told me where he'd be.

As long as it didn't explode, we were good.

"*Quaerere dominum.*" I spoke in a commanding, no-nonsense voice and sent magic into the jacket as I said the words.

Seconds later, a light appeared in midair. A line, sort of like it was made from a neon sign. Only I could see it. "Let's go. Wherever he is, he's not somewhere guarded." Magic could be done to make a location unsearchable. My home had been protected that way probably since the day it was originally built. That reminded me, I needed to refresh that spell.

Spells didn't last forever, though I suspected the house wouldn't let its inhabitants be found... or messed with.

"Come on," I said urgently, walking toward the front door and grabbing my coat on the way. The line of light preceded me, directing me to Zane.

I stepped out to see the Johnson's had an SUV. "Oh, good, can you drive?" I asked. We'd all fit in it.

They ran out ahead of me, and Olivia and Owen followed. I ran back inside and yelled up the stairs. "Back in a while!"

"Okay," Larry called down. "Be careful."

Seconds later, I was in the passenger seat, giving directions to Rick. "I have no idea how far it will take us," I said. "This sort of locator spell isn't like when you do a scry over a map." I described the light I saw and how we were following it. We drove down the coast road for a good ten minutes before anything changed. "Hang on," I barked. "Turn here." The light veered off to the right.

"There's no road," Rick said. "Just a field."

"Well, go as far as you can in the vehicle, then we'll walk."

Olivia leaned forward. "There's not a road nearby that I know of. This is a bunch of woods, owned by the government if I'm not mistaken."

"Text Sam," I said. "Let him know what we're doing."

Rick pulled off the road and drove carefully across the field, getting close to the copse of trees. "Now what?"

"Let's go." I unbuckled my seatbelt. "We might be walking a while. I can't tell."

We didn't end up having to walk far before the light blinked and faded. "It's gone," I whispered.

"What does that mean?" Rick spoke in a hushed voice. Something about the woods made us all feel like someone was looking over our shoulders.

"Either someone intercepted our spell," Owen said. "Or Zane crossed onto spelled land where he can't be tracked. Given where the spell took us, I'm guessing he's on spelled land now."

"Let's keep going forward," I said. "Maybe we'll get lucky."

As we walked, hope began to wane.

And then, a noise. I held up my hand and

everyone froze. "I heard something," I said in a hushed voice.

Very carefully, we tiptoed forward until a clearing came into view behind the trees. There was an old horse paddock, what looked like pig pens, and a barn. Farther back, near the other side of the clearing, was a small shed.

A small service road led off into the forest on the opposite side. As we stood looking around, the sound of a vehicle starting made us all duck, but it was parked out of sight down that road because we never saw it leave as the sound of the engine faded.

After another several minutes, when nobody came out of the barn and nothing seemed to move, we tiptoed out of the woods and toward the big, faded red structure.

We circled the barn, but the only door was inside the horse paddock. Pushing open the gate, I tiptoed into the big circle and moved quickly toward the barn door.

"I smell him!" Rick rushed around me and pulled the door open, despite my hurried whisper for him to wait. Dana followed quickly behind.

We followed on their heels, not that I could've stopped Dana from going to her son once they had a line on him.

The interior of the barn was dim; the only light was from a few missing boards over the windows in the loft area. The ground was dirt and hay. There were three stalls on each side.

We found the poor shifter kids in one of the horse stalls, huddled in the corner. "Mama," one little boy cried and ran forward. "Papa!"

I smiled as Dana and Rick got their son back, exclaiming in relief to see him, then we entered the stall, and my smile faded. These kids had gone through hell. It made my heart ache to think about it. Well, we were here now, and they'd never have to fight again.

Olivia and I crouched down. "Hi," I said softly. "Are you guys okay?"

A teenage girl stepped forward. "We're hungry, but everyone here healed from the last fight." A tear tracked down her face. "We don't know where the shifters who lost the fights went."

My chest tightened even more while my magic roared to life deep inside me. I was going to make whoever was responsible for this to pay. Long and painful.

"Well, we'll figure all that out," Olivia said. "Let's get you out of here."

"The bad man just left," Zane said as we helped kids of various ages off the dirty ground.

While I took calming breaths, I ran around to inspect the rest of the barn and make sure nobody else was hiding anywhere. "Is there anyone else we need to look for?"

"No, they usually had us fight other real animals like dogs or roosters," the teen girl said.

"What's your name, honey?" Olivia asked.

"Jennifer-Nicole," she said. "I'm a wolf shifter"

"Adams?" Rick asked.

Jennifer-Nicole nodded, her eyes brightening a little with the hope that someone knew her. "Yeah."

"I know your parents." He held one arm out, and she gratefully cradled herself under in his arms as tears fell. "Let's get you home to them, okay?"

Sniffling, we led the kids out of the pen. Well, Olivia was sniffling, I was blinking back tears while counting all the ways to make everyone involved in this pay. Both alive and dead. I wasn't the type to wish ill on anyone, but what I saw and heard since raising little Ricky made me rethink some of my morals. Some people just plain sucked and needed to be introduced to Luci.

"We're going to have to get creative to fit all six of these kids in that SUV," I whispered to Olivia.

"We'll call Sam to come help as soon as we get far enough away," Olivia said. "We've got to get them out of here."

I picked up a little girl who was sniffling and shaking, then set her back down. After wrapping her in my jacket, I pulled her back into my arms and cradled her close. "Hey, sweet girl. How old are you?"

"Seven," she whispered.

Holy crap. She was so small, about the size of Sammie, who was five. "How long have you been there?"

She shrugged and burrowed into my coat. The poor girl stunk to the high heavens, but I'd never tell her that. "I think two years."

My throat squeezed. "Have you fought all that time?"

She nodded. "I'm a panther. I have very sharp claws."

Oh, no. This poor child. I closed my eyes and prayed to the goddess to give me the strength to get through this.

Warmth enveloped us, and I turned my head to smile at Owen. He'd given us a spell to keep all of us warm as we walked. The kids certainly needed it.

He had a little boy in his arms, too.

"Clear," Dana whispered after she and Zane peered out of the barn.

We rushed across the field the way we came, not going as fast as I liked, but there were more kids than adults. Many of the kids were weak from lack of food and fighting for their life.

When we reached the trees, Owen moved closer to me. "Do you feel that?"

"Yeah. Can you tell what it is?" A low pulse of magic nipped at my skin, but I couldn't tell what it was or where it was coming from.

"You're the witch." He flashed me a grin even though there wasn't much humor in it.

"Half witch." I sat the little girl down on her feet and tugged my jacket tight around her, buttoning the top button. "Why don't you run up ahead and see if there is anything in the forest. I'll scan the area with my *witchy* powers."

Owen eyed me and handed the little boy over to Olivia. "If I die, I'll come back to haunt you."

I flashed him a smile. "Only if I don't heal you first or turn you into a ghoul. Whatever works."

He grumbled something as he walked forward holding out his hands like he's walking in the dark. Olivia snickered beside me. "What is he doing?"

"Feeling around in the dark, what else?"

Dana moved into the spot Owen just vacated. "What's going on?"

"We sense magic but don't know where it's coming from." Which was odd. I should have been able to pinpoint the source.

Opening my senses, I searched the area for magic, stretching my magic out. It didn't go far before it bounced back to me, catching me off guard. I gasped and cut my flow of energy.

Olivia placed a hand on my arm. "What's wrong."

Owen yelled back at us at the same time I answered her question. "There is a magic barrier." I sighed and added, "We're trapped unless we can figure out how to get out."

"Can we just run through it?" Olivia asked. "Maybe with all of us rushing at it at the same time will weaken it or break it altogether."

I glanced at Owen, who had returned from his short walk. He shrugged. "We could try. I hit it with my fist a few times and it rippled."

"Okay." I met Dana's and Rick's gazes then the kids. "I think the kids should move back a little."

Zane and Jennifer-Nicole gathered the kids in a group and directed them back a few feet. Then they returned to our side. Zane lifted his head high. "We will help."

I was about to say no way, but Zane's dad studied the two of them. "Are you sure? It'll hurt a lot if the barrier holds."

Jennifer-Nicole shrugged. "I've felt worse."

I locked my jaw and turned away from her. The grandmaster of the fighting ring was going to suffer.

"Okay let's do this." Olivia bounced on her feet, making me snicker.

"On the count of three," I said.

Owen started the countdown. "One."

"Two."

We all said three at the same and ran right into the barrier a few feet ahead. We didn't bounce off the magic wall as much as we were thrown a few yards back. My body seized as an electrical current shot through me. When we landed, I was sure we were all going to die.

CHAPTER NINETEEN

a jangling sound brought me to my feet and put me on alert. We'd been sitting in the shade of the barn for a while, comfortable, at least, thanks to Owen's warmth bubble. He and I had been steadily shooting magic at the barrier, trying to weaken it or, ideally, bring it down.

Nothing worked.

But now, someone was here. And I had to prepare to defend myself and the kids against whoever or whatever might be coming our way.

We'd talked about using our necromancer powers to try to raise something nearby, but we'd decided against it for a couple of reasons, one of which being what if we raised one of the poor kids who had already died?

What these poor littles had been through was bad enough. They didn't need to see the reanimated corpses of their friends.

Though, that would be a chore for me and Owen later down the road. Any shifter child still missing would have to be found. How we'd do it without bringing up every legitimate dead person, I had no idea.

We'd figure it out. Because their families needed closure.

A person stepped around the barn, and I squinted against the sunlight at their back.

"Howdy, pardner," the man drawled.

I gasped and dropped the hand shielding my eyes. "Luci?"

He walked forward so the sun no longer blinded me and grinned broadly. "Heard you needed a rescue."

Turning in a slow circle, he allowed us to take in his getup. He'd dressed like a stereotypical cowboy, from the pristine white ten-gallon hat to the spurs. He even had a six-shooter on his hip.

"Luci, my friend," I said. "I'm beyond glad to see you, but you look absolutely ridiculous."

He chuckled and snapped his fingers, his normal suit and tie returning. "Better?" He'd kept the hat.

"Much. Can you get us out of here?" I threw a rock toward the barrier to show how it rippled with magic, only visible for a brief few seconds.

"I intercepted your attempts to get in touch with your fellow humans," he said. "Good thing, too."

Bending over, he peered through the paddock slats at the children. "What have we here? Kiddos? I love the young!" He beamed at the huddling shifters behind us. "I'm Luci, my little appetizers. How are you?"

Jennifer-Nicole stepped forward. "Scared. Can you get us out of here?" Brave girl. She tossed her red hair over her shoulder and stared at Luci.

The grin on Luci's face faltered. "My, my. You've been through quite the ordeal, haven't you?" He squinted at Jennifer-Nicole. "You have my solemn vow, my little snack-sized human. Your tormentors will suffer."

She cocked her head as she studied him. "You have a lot of power?"

Luci spread his arms and straightened up. "The most."

"Please, take me home to my mother," she whispered.

Luci winked at us, then spread his hand out in midair. He stroked the air as if caressing a lover, but I knew he was getting the makeup of the ward to bring it down. "Clever," he whispered. "This ward is specially made to make sure nobody outside it could sense the torment inside. It wasn't, however, made to contain a full-blooded witch, which is why you were able to signal me."

I hadn't even thought of signaling him. Not that I would've anyway. He was still too much of an anomaly. And not on my hero call list.

"It was also not made to withstand me." He grinned again, straightened his tie, then snapped his finger once. "All clear. Let's go find our bad guys."

"Now hang on," I cried, rushing toward the paddock gate on the other side of the barn. "You can't go rushing off to attack whoever did this. We don't have enough information."

"Silly woman," Luci thundered. "I am the de—"

"Dear friend of the coven, I know," I said hastily. These kids had no idea Luci was the devil. And no way did I want them to find out.

"And the best *witch* in town," he said darkly, then turned to the kids. "Come on out of there."

I wasn't sure I liked the way he looked at the kids like he couldn't decide if he wanted to make them soldiers in his Hell army or cook them for dinner.

Over my dead body *and* my ghost once he killed me for protecting the little angel warriors.

Turning to the adults, I said, "Get the kids out of here. It might be easier to take them to my house and have the parents come there." My house was warded to protect the innocent. It would save us a bit of gas and time. "Plus, they can shower or bathe while waiting for their parents."

Olivia nodded. "I'll call Carrie to see if she could bring some clothes over for them. There should be some in the school lost and found."

Rick said, "We can take those who are close to our pack."

"I can run out to the second-hand shop in town and pick up some things, too," Dana added, in full momma shifter mode.

It was great to know they had everything under control.

"Carrie is at my house," Luci offered with a sly grin.

I opened my mouth, then closed it. I wasn't going to ask. None of my business. Not to mention, I was sure Olivia would ask Carrie a butt load of questions when she got there.

As the kids disappeared through the trees, I turned and glared at Luci. "Now, listen," I said, wagging my finger at him. "No charging off without me. We need to do this right, so we get to the bottom of the whole mess. This is no one-man operation."

Luci glowered. "This isn't my first investigation, Ava. I am the devil, after all."

"Yes, and as such, you're used to getting your way and going in guns blazing. We do this my way."

He twinkled his eyes at me as if tolerating my insubordination. My stomach churned, knowing I was out here in the middle of nowhere alone with him. As attractive as he was, knowing what he was made it impossible for me to be anything but nervous. But I damn sure wasn't going to show it.

"Let's check out the barn with a better light source," I said. "Then that shed."

He led the way and created a glaring ball of light, throwing it up to hang in the eaves of the barn. "I'll go left, you go right."

With a sharp nod, I inspected each stall on the right. They stunk, and both animal and human feces were piled in the corner of each. Wishing I knew a spell to remove the sense of smell, I burrowed my nose in my shirt and moved quickly, scanning the dirt floor for any sign of any clue.

There was nothing. And as disappointed as I was

that we still had no idea who had done this, I was more than ready to get out of the barn.

We exited the back of the barn, that door opening easily now that the ward was down, and walked around the outside, Luci again going left while I went right. The ground was clean, the dirt smooth and trackless. My shoes left footprints, so whoever had driven away just before we got here must've done something to remove their tracks.

"Shed?" I asked when Luci and I met around the paddock.

He looked around. "Unless there are more buildings in the woods, it seems the shed is our only other recourse."

We fanned out and walked across a small dirt clearing to the woodshed. Something glinted in the sunlight near the door. "Hang on," I said, hurrying forward.

I bent and picked up the object, gasping as I wiped off the metal. "I don't believe it."

The circular item was a coin, and it had been stamped similarly to the coins found on all the murder victims. "We've got to get Drew out here," I murmured. "I think this is going to be bigger than shifter kids."

"Don't shifters avoid human police interception?" Luci asked. "They keep to themselves."

"They do, but this looks like a half-stamped coin just like the ones we've been finding in pockets of murder victims." Including my mother.

"Then, by all means, let's get into this shed," Luci said.

We hurried toward the door, but about the time Luci reached out for the padlock, the sound of a vehicle on the road reached my ears. Luci heard it a few seconds before I did because his head swung around toward the lane, and he froze.

"Out of sight," Luci hissed before grabbing my arm and pulling me around the back of the shed. "Let's see who I get to kill today."

"Stop," I whispered, slapping his arm. "You're not killing anyone. We might need whoever it is to give us information about the murderers."

"You're no fun," he whispered in my ear, making me shiver.

We stood behind the shed and peered around the corner, covered by a large bush, as a small silver sedan parked behind the barn.

"No way." To my complete, utter, devastating shock, Penny stepped out of the car.

Penny! The woman whose husband had died

just before Halloween, killed by Carmen Moon-flower. Her husband, William—Bill—had been a necromancer and the original owner of Alfred.

What in the world was she doing here?

"Stop, foul beast!" Luci yelled as he ran out from around the shed.

Oh, damn it. Why'd he have to be so dramatic? I hurried after him. "Don't hurt her," I called. "I know her."

Catching up, I yanked on his arm. He was pointing a potent finger at my Yaya's lifelong friend as I felt his power increasing. I stepped in front of him, drawing his attention to me. "Hang on, Luci. Let her explain."

Penny stared at us with her jaw hinged open. "Ava." Her voice squeaked and her eyes rounded as she stared at me and then Luci. "What are you doing here?"

"Looking for the missing shifters," I said with the calm I didn't feel. "How can you be involved in something like this?" *Please have a reasonable excuse.*

Penny was the sweetest person I'd ever met. Or at least I'd thought she was. It broke my heart that she would have anything to do with the cruelty that had gone on here.

"I'm not," she stuttered. "I'm doing the same thing."

I gave her a flat look and Luci scoffed. "A likely excuse. Care to elaborate?"

"I know a shifter family and they asked me to find their daughter," she said. "I did a locator spell that led me here."

I knew she was lying as much as I knew my own name. But I had no proof. "I'm sorry, Penny, but we can't let you walk away from here on just that information."

But what to do with her? "Luci, can you put her in the barn and put up a ward so she can't get out?" I asked.

He gave me a low bow. "I live to serve her majesty necromancer."

But I didn't miss the scathing look that accompanied that bow. He didn't like me taking charge. He'd tolerated it for a while, but his patience was waning.

Well, that was too dang bad. We were here on my dime right now. As appreciative as I was that he'd rescued us, I had to do this right or the people behind the fighting ring might get away.

"Thank you," I said stiffly.

I searched through Penny's car but didn't find anything. With no way of knowing if Olivia and

Owen had made it back to the car yet to call Sam and Drew, I had to decide if we should wait here for them or take Penny's car back to my house and wait.

If nothing else, I wanted to see what was in that shed. With the half-pressed coin outside it, surely there was something good inside.

Luci walked out of the barn and straightened his suit. "Well, as you seem to have things in order, and a vehicle to get yourself back to your home, I'm going to leave you to it."

"Hang on," I said, but he held up a hand.

"No, you're doing so well on your own that you don't need me." He sniffed. "The ward on the barn will disintegrate if you walk through it. Only you. So *don't* do that unless you're ready for Miss Penny to leave with you."

Crap. I'd offended him by taking the lead. "No, I'm sorry."

Luci grinned at me with that familiar mischievous glint in his eyes. "Don't be sorry. But I'll see you later."

With a snap, he disappeared, leaving me with Penny locked in the barn and no clue what to do next.

I pulled out my phone and realized it had no service. Ugh. I walked away from the barn hoping to get a signal, but with no luck. They must have had a spell for that, too.

The rumbling of a car engine made my pulse increase. I whirled around and blew out a breath in relief to see Drew's cruiser driving down the service road.

When I reached the barn, he and Sam stepped out of the police car. I wasn't sure how much Olivia had told them, so I recapped and filled them in about Penny. "I can't believe she's involved with something like this."

"You'd be surprised what people are capable of." Drew reached out for me, and I took his hand and allowed him to pull me into a hug. "How are you?"

"Sad and disgusted." I breathed him in and instantly relaxed. I enjoyed the feeling of being wrapped in his warmth a little longer, then stepped back. "I have the kids at my house. Or did I say that already?"

I was so tired I was repeating myself.

Drew touched my cheek. When I raised my gaze to his, he said, "Let Penny out so we can take her in, then go take care of the kids."

Nodding, I pressed a kiss to his cheek before leading them inside the barn. Just as Luci said, the ward holding Penny broke as soon as I walked through it. Not able to look at the older woman, I left her in Drew and Sam's care.

When I drove onto the main road, my cell worked, so I texted Olivia to pick me up at Penny's house. I had to take her car back anyway so the neighbors wouldn't ask too many questions.

On the way to my house, I was having Olivia stop off at the liquor store so I could grab a bottle of wine. I was going to need it after this day was through.

CHAPTER TWENTY

*O*wen picked me up from Penny's. "Olivia is holding down the fort. Alfred didn't know what to do with all those kids, so he took Larry upstairs. So, I think we are on our own for dinner. Also, I think Snooze packed up and left."

A laugh burst from my lips. "Did you actually see Snooze pack up?"

He chuckled. "No, but he had his favorite toy in his mouth as he ran out the back door."

"He'll be back." I was still smiling at the thought of my fat, immortal cat running away from home just because of a bunch of kids when we pulled into my driveway. There were a few cars I didn't recognize parked out front. Must be parents picking up kids.

Before getting out of the car, I said, "I want to go back to see if we can get into that shed. Lucifer and I didn't get a chance to check it out before Penny showed."

"I'll go with you."

I was hoping he would offer. Sam was going too. He just didn't know it yet. I wanted a bit of police presence at the scene.

Inside my old, cranky house was a form of organized chaos I wouldn't have believed if I hadn't seen it. The coffee table had been loaded down with snacks, both junk food and healthy fruit. There was even a veggie tray and cheese platter. A few of the younger kids were on the sofa watching a cartoon on TV, while a couple of kids at the dining table sat with plates of food. One, a little girl, was on the phone most likely talking to her parents from the way tears filled her eyes as she smiled.

It'd been a long time since these kids smiled.

And I wasn't going to think about that. They were free from evil and going home to their parents.

Carrie emerged from the hallway carrying a clean and adorable little boy. His name was Sammie and looked just like my childhood BFF. Carrie smiled at me. "Welcome to Ava's shifter day camp."

"It sure looks like one. Where did the food come

from?" I loved junk food as much as a college student, but I didn't remember half the stuff in the coffee table spread.

"I picked it up on my way over." Carrie walked to the sofa and sat down while drying off Sammie. Owen had gone up to his room to get out of everyone's hair, his words. I had a suspicion he wasn't comfortable around so many kids. Although he'd been great with them at the barn.

"Thanks for coming to help out." Voices in the kitchen drew my curiosity so I thought I'd check it out.

Olivia was in there with someone's parents, talking privately, out of earshot of little ears. She looked over and introduced me to the parents. "This is Ava Harper. She discovered the...where the kids were."

The last part of the statement held sadness and anger. I've never heard outright anger come from Olivia. Not even when we didn't like each other in high school. Holding out my hand, I shook the mother's then the father's. "I'm a mom, too, but I could only imagine what you and the other parents went through."

That was when I noticed more parents out on the back porch.

"I'm Nick and this is my mate, Ashley," The father said as he took my hand and held it a little longer than I expected. "We're Jennifer-Nicole's parents. We had to come and thank you in person. If you ever need anything, just call."

"I was just doing what I felt was the right thing. I do have to tell you that the police have one suspect in custody. The kids said she brought them food." I'd found dog food in the car. It turned my stomach to think the kids would eat that or starve.

"Why the police?" Nick's voice took on an alpha tone, which I ignored.

Locking gazes with him, I said, "The fighting ring is connected to a serial murder case. The sheriff and the deputy know about the paranormal world and are working on concealing the supernatural part of it from human notice." In fact, the paranormal aspects of the investigation were completely off record. As far as the record was concerned, all the deaths had been run-of-the-mill human psychopath murders. But I didn't need to tell them that. There were too many questions that needed to be answered first.

The alpha wolf gave me a short nod, but I could tell he wasn't happy about it. Tough. This was my rodeo and I'd do what I want. Including using the help of the police.

Suddenly something hit my side and latched on. I wrapped an arm around the sweet teen and hugged her close. She smelled of apples and spring air and her hair was still damp. "How are you?"

Jennifer-Nicole flashed me a smile. "Much better. Thanks to you."

"Hey, I didn't work alone." I rubbed her shoulder and squeezed her tight.

"Well, thank you and everyone who helped save us." Then she darted out the back door, followed by her parents. My gaze moved to the conservatory, relieved it was closed off to the kids. I didn't need them getting into anything in there, especially the poisonous plants.

I spent the next few hours talking with parents as they collected their kiddos and took them home.

After my house was mine again, I sat on the sofa and took a piece of cheese from the platter. "Owen, Sam, and I are going back to check out the shed."

Olivia sat beside me. Carrie had left about thirty minutes ago. After a few seconds, Olivia said, "I'll need to take Sammie home to put him to bed. He has school tomorrow."

I glanced outside through the window and

frowned. The sun had begun to set. "I hadn't realized it was so late."

Olivia's phone chimed. When she looked at it, she giggled. "Does Sam know he's going with you?"

"No." I grinned.

That made her laugh. "I'll inform him he's been voluntold that he's going."

"You do that. I'm going to shower and change."

Olivia stood and called to Sammie, telling him it was time to go home. Moments later Alfred descended the stairs with a sleeping little boy in his arms. Taking her son from Alfred, Olivia, said, "Thanks, Alfie."

The ghoul grunted and then handed me his tablet. One word was typed in. **Dinner.**

"No. Owen and I will be leaving when Sam gets here so we'll pick something up.

Alfred looked put out that he couldn't cook, which made me laugh. The ghoul didn't even eat. "Alfie, thank you for everything you do."

His features softened without actually softening, and he nodded before going back upstairs. I had a great group of friends and family. With all the twists and turns my life had, I needed these people to keep me semi-sane.

When Olivia went out the door, Drew came in. I frowned. "Why are you here?"

"To go back to the barn with you."

"Okay, great." I guessed Sam wanted to hold his son and be with Olivia. Who could blame him after seeing what we did today? "Owen, you ready?" I called up the stairs.

"I'm right here. You don't need to yell."

I jumped and whirled around. He stood in the archway to the kitchen with a half-eaten sandwich in his hand. "Geesh. I didn't even see you come down."

We piled into Dia, my Hyundai, and drove out to the site. This time I knew where the service road was, so we didn't have to walk through the woods.

It was a wasted trip. The darn shed was magically sealed. Nothing Owen or I tried worked to break the spell. Drew even tried old-fashioned brute strength. He kicked the door, rammed into it with his shoulder, and even shot it. Nothing worked.

I needed witches for this. After all, it had been a witch who'd cursed the coins. With Penny involved, it made more sense it was a *local* witch. I just had to come up with a plan to fish the murderer out.

After returned to my house, I called Sam and Olivia and put them on speaker. Owen, Drew and I were in the conservatory because I'd found a truth serum recipe. I was cooking up the serum while we planned our next move.

"We are sure the murderer is a witch," Sam said.

I nodded, agreeing with him. "It has to be. It doesn't take a lot of power to curse something, but whoever was doing it would have to know how to create a curse and it takes magic that only a born witch has. Humans who study witchcraft don't have the natural magic in their blood to activate the curse."

I stood a little straighter because I'd actually known that one. Mainly because I read it in one of the grimoires the other day, but I didn't have to tell them.

"Right. The only way to activate a curse is with witch blood," Owen added.

"So it has to be someone in the coven," Olivia said. "That would make sense because only coven members were killed."

My thoughts exactly. "So we need to set a trap. What better way than a coven field trip?"

I poured the serum into an amber-colored jar and sat it in the window where it would get the morning sun. Unfortunately, as tended to be with these things, it took a week to mature. We were on our own until then. If I found myself in any real danger, as long as I was close enough to a cemetery, I could defend myself and mine, but out in the woods like that? I wasn't sure if my witch side could step up to the occasion. Even though I was supposed to be all-powerful, I didn't feel like it. I wasn't ready to test the theory either.

CHAPTER TWENTY-ONE

*B*right and early the next afternoon, I drafted a letter and sent it to every member of the coven I knew. Owen helped me use their names and the internet to find addresses for each of them. If we did our spell right, they'd get the letter and come to my home this evening for an emergency coven meeting.

As the unofficial leader of the coven, I had every right to call such a meeting, but to them, I was a newbie among their ranks. CeCe had told me I would be the new leader in secret, so I assumed none of the other members knew. I wasn't sure how any of that worked.

Someone was bound to know now that CeCe

was dead. Either way, the members would be too intrigued to pass up the invite. At least I hoped so.

Since we had hours before the coven would arrive, if they did, Owen and I traipsed out into the woods past Luci's house.

I'd wanted to go straight back to the barn where we'd found the children and start looking for buried bodies, but Owen and Drew and Sam *and* Olivia had all advised against it until we had a better idea of who was doing this.

Although, I wasn't against seeing the corpse of a big bear or mountain lion go after whoever had done this to these poor shifter babies, I couldn't be sure there'd be enough for me to raise way out there. The bones had to be close enough to the surface.

So, Owen and I were going to practice near my house and see if I could bring up any more animals here. One shifter had already been found buried in these woods. Why not more?

We returned to the same clearing we'd found Ricky in, and I began. For hours, I expanded my reach, raising anything I found and drawing them to me.

I got a lot more than I bargained for.

"Whoa," Owen said when I stopped to rest. All around us, animal carcasses laid, at rest once more, in circles going across the field. "We're going to have to rebury all these animals."

We hadn't come across any more shifters. Just more bunnies, birds, and squirrels. A few skunks, a fox, and three deer. "I'm going to try one more time," I said. "I'm getting miles out now."

Owen shook his head. "I've never seen anything like this, Ava. You're more powerful than we ever knew. I don't think we ever really tried to test you like this."

I opened one eye and squinted at him. "Now we know."

I was just as shocked as he was.

What we'd do with it after this? I had no idea. What good was a necromancer, really? I had no plans to use my powers for evil. What could I do with them?

After my brief break, I closed my eyes and searched farther out. "Oh," I gasped. "I can feel the difference. There's a human."

"Can you go over it?" he asked.

I shook my head. "No. If I'm right about its location, it's not buried in a cemetery."

He sighed. "Make him hide himself on his way," he urged. "We don't want anyone seeing a dead body walking around. The animals are bad enough."

I chuckled and did as he asked. It took nearly an hour for the skeleton to get to us. As she neared, I felt her, knew she was female, and when she was very close, I could tell stuff like the age of the body. "No," I said. "She's too old."

A skeleton walked into the clearing. If I hadn't been able to feel the difference, I would've thought it was Larry just by looking at her. I couldn't tell the difference in bones from a male or a female. I wasn't a doctor, after all. Or a bone scientist. Who knew about bones? Anthropologist, probably.

"Hello," I said.

The skeleton walked closer. "Hello," she whispered. "How am I here?"

"I'm trying to find anyone who was killed, murdered," I said. "Were you?"

She sighed and looked up at the trees. "When is this?"

I didn't want to freak her out. "When did you die?"

Her white head, smudged with dirt, moved around as she took in our surroundings. "I believe it was 1966."

Owen and I exchanged a glance. That was when our witchy serial killer was getting started. "Do you know how you died?" I asked.

"It was an accident," she said. "But then, after I died, someone in a hood came and buried me in the woods. Why would he do that if it was an accident?" Her wispy voice sounded far away. Nowhere near as strong as Larry. I wondered if it was the twenty years that made a difference.

"Are you at peace?" I asked.

She nodded. "I was. My parents came to me recently. We moved on together."

"Can you tell me anything about how you died?" I asked. "Or your name?"

"My name was Megan Frey," she said. "And I died cutting through a big field, going to school. I was bitten by a snake, but I'd left late for school and nobody heard me yelling."

"A snake," I gasped. "That's horrible."

She nodded. "Yes. I'd like to go back to my parents now, please."

"Of course, dear." I gestured to an empty spot on the grass. "Please, lay down."

Pulling my magic back the way Owen had taught me, I let sweet Megan go back to her peace.

"Well," Owen said. "We don't know if she was killed by our serial killer, but it's apparent we have a lot of work to do. I think it's time I helped instead of trying to teach you."

I squinted up at the sky. "Yes, but for now we have to get back."

We rushed back to the house, leaving all the bones in the clearing for now. We had to get Sam and Drew in on the skeleton mess. I was fairly sure I could lead them to her gravesite, which might pick up more clues for us.

I hoped.

"We took longer than I thought," I said, breathless from running back home. I needed to start working out. I laughed at that thought. Yeah, right. That would be the day.

"We'll barely have time to clean up," Owen said. "But I think we'll make it."

Before we left, we'd asked Alfred to make finger foods for our guests, and Larry had been excited to help.

Once we had the murderer, I was going to be sad to see Larry go. He was a sweet house guest, if odd at times.

As it turned out, we didn't have time to clean up at all. As we rounded the house, Bevan Magnus stood from my porch swing. Figures that weasel would be the first one there.

"There you are," he called, holding up the letter I'd sent to him. His expression told me he resented that I'd summoned him and the rest of the coven. "How dare you call an emergency coven meeting?"

Yep, he was pissy about it. And he'd have to get over it.

I almost apologized as I walked up my porch steps. Almost. Luckily, I came to my senses. He didn't deserve my apology after turning his nose up at me the two previous times we'd met. I plastered a fake smile on and said, "Please, come in."

Hopefully, I'd sent enough invitations to other coven members that he wouldn't be the only one to show up.

He gave me the willies.

Bevan followed me in the door. I wasn't sure if he'd been at the Christmas party or not. There'd been so many people in and out of the house then, there was no telling. But the way he looked around in interest made me think he hadn't come.

Alfred shuffled out of the kitchen holding a tray with lemonade.

"Please," I said again, a fake smile still intact. "Sit in the living room and enjoy a drink. Owen and I will be right back down. I just want to wash this dirt off."

"Of course," Bevan said, staring at Alfred with wide eyes.

I started up the stairs, but when I heard the tell-tale clack of Larry's bony feet on the hardwood floor, I stopped and turned. Pressing my lips into a thin line, I tried to keep in the giggle that bubbled up.

The skeleton walked into the living room carrying a tray as Owen and I watched on. "Hello, I'm Larry."

Bevan, just in my line of sight in one of the high-back chairs, paled considerably. "He-hello."

Owen started to chuckle, and I elbowed him. If he started laughing, there was no stopping me.

"Can I interest you in a finger sandwich?" Larry asked and bent over.

"Sure," Bevan whispered and took one. I couldn't tell for sure from this far away, but I thought his hand trembled. "Larry, you say?"

"Yes. I was murdered in the eighties," he said matter of factly, studying Bevan with interest. "You seem familiar. Perhaps we knew one another."

"I don't think so." Bevan took a bite, but his gaze kept darting up at Alfred and Larry, bouncing between them like he was watching a tennis match. He swallowed hard, but then I tiptoed on up the stairs, followed by Owen.

As soon as we hit the upstairs landing, we fell all over each other in laughter.

And the doorbell rang. Crap. "Don't get that," I called to Alfred. Just in case it wasn't a witch. "Glamour?" I asked Owen.

He shrugged. We certainly didn't have time to shower now. We both ran our hands over our faces, hiding the dirt. Seconds later, Owen's black hair was shiny and clean, and his face looked like it had been scrubbed pink.

"Perfect," I whispered. "Let's go."

When I opened the door, all of the rest of the coven stood on my porch. "Oh," I whispered. "Hi."

I shook each of their hands as they walked in. "Please," I called before they started in. "Go into the living room. We've got refreshments and I've had my house ghoul bring plenty of seats in."

"Hello, Melody, Cade." I shook Melody's hand as she walked past.

"Leena, Mai." Nodding at them, I smiled encouragingly.

"Thank you for coming, Joely." She beamed at me, her rosy cheeks always cheerful looking.

"Alissa, you look nice." I smiled at one of the younger members of the coven, then turned to the last two. "Brandon, Ben, thanks for coming."

The nearly elderly twins came through last, and

I shut the door behind them. Ben hung back. "You have a house ghoul?" he whispered.

"Oh, yes, Alfred. I inherited him from Billy Combs when he died."

Ben's eyes widened. "Impressive."

"Hello, everyone, and thank you for coming. Please, have lemonade, or..." I gestured toward Alfred. "Alfie here will be coming around with plain iced water if you prefer."

Alfred nodded once. I noticed he'd come up with a rather lumpy-looking brown suit from somewhere. How sweet. He wanted to look nice for our company.

"I brought you all here today because a great tragedy has occurred in our community." I met their eyes one by one. "Someone has been running a shifter fighting ring right in our backyard."

Ben and Brandon's faces registered pure shock, as did Leena and Melody. Bevan's eyes darkened and his mouth thinned into a line.

Interesting. He'd creeped me out all along. Maybe he was involved.

Mai raised her hand. "That's horrible, but what does it have to do with us?"

"The police are working with the shifter community to find the people responsible for this travesty," I said. "But there is a shed on the property that has been magically locked. I can't get it open on my own. I need your help."

"Absolutely not," Ben said. "This is shifter business. Shifters do not like interference."

I raised my eyebrow at him. Why such a strong opposing opinion? "This is far beyond a shifter problem," I said. I didn't want to tell them, yet we suspected the murderer in our town was related to the shifter ring.

Ben harrumphed as Brandon shook his head. "The shifters become hostile when we interfere. We've tried it before."

"Not this time," I said. "This time, they need our help." Plus, I guessed by finding the kids, I'd made some kind of alliance with the shifters. Again, though, that was not information I was ready to share with the coven. Not until I weeded out the killer.

CHAPTER TWENTY-TWO

We piled into three cars, with me driving one, Bevan driving his monstrous SUV, and Alissa driving her minivan. She looked like a soccer mom, so it made sense.

Drew had been on standby to meet us out there, so I texted him when we left my house.

The sun had begun its late afternoon descent by the time we pulled in, but we still had a couple of hours of light left before it was totally dark.

I smiled when I saw Drew leaning against his patrol car. His ankles were crossed, and he looked hot. Sexy, not temperature. My heart did its little rapid beats as we locked gazes.

Once everyone was out of the cars, I introduced the sheriff. "Everyone, this is Drew."

He stepped around his cruiser and joined me by my car as everyone gathered around. Olivia was going to plotz when I told her about all this. She'd be so mad she wasn't here.

"And this is Sam," Olivia's voice chirped. She and Sam came walking out of the barn. That little turd. She'd convinced them to let her come. I couldn't help but grin at my best friend. Sneaky little she-devil. At some point, she'd taken Sam's place as confidante numero uno in my life. And I was okay with that.

"What is the meaning of this?" Bevan hissed.

"It's okay, everyone. Sam has known about witchcraft since we were kids. We grew up together. And Olivia also knows. They're not going to blow our cover." I rolled my eyes. I was pretty sure the whole town knew I was a witch. It was partly why I loved Shipton Harbor so much.

The coven studied them with guarded, suspicious eyes, then as one unit, turned their attention to Drew. I caught a few reactions that were covered up. They suspected he was a hunter.

I'd felt it when we first met, too. Something about him wasn't quite human and I'd recognized it. Of course, I hadn't known about hunters at the time and didn't know what he was from the magical energy surrounding him. But the coven members *would* know about hunters.

"And Drew..." I waited a brief few seconds. "Drew comes from a long line of hunters." They'd figure it out anyway. Might as well be honest.

Drew grimaced as the witches gasped and backed away. "No," he said swiftly. "It's okay. I rejected that part of my life. I can't say I wouldn't take down an *evil* supernatural creature, but I'm not hunting innocent witches or shifters or anyone. Most of us just want to live our lives."

Everyone stopped moving backward, at least. Nobody was overly excited to have Drew, Olivia, or Sam here, but at least they'd stopped looking terrified.

"Anyway," I said. "This is the shed we need to be opened. I was thinking if everyone touched it and said the same spell, maybe we could get it open."

Bevan sighed. "It might work."

I arched an eyebrow at him. "Do you mind helping?"

He dipped his head toward me. "Not a'tall."

Creepy little effer.

We walked to the shed, and the coven lined up alongside it, each of them placing two hands on it.

"Okay, everyone, just use a simple unlocking incantation," I said.

"*Intrabit* should do the trick," Owen called down the side of the shed. Everyone nodded, most of us being familiar with the simple spell. It wasn't the spell itself that would do the trick, it was our combined power.

But no matter how hard or how much power I sent into the shed, it wouldn't open. "It feels like someone is working against us," I muttered lower enough only Owen heard me.

He nodded. "Let's take a break," he called. "Could half of you come with me?" He pointed to a few of the coven, including Bevan and the twins. "I need help with something in the barn."

I wiped imaginary sweat off my brow. "I'm going to rest a minute and we'll try again when you get back."

Relief flowed in my veins when no one in the group complained, much. Bevan did glare at me as he walked away.

When they disappeared into the barn, I sighed and looked at the shed. "Come on, let's give it a shot," I said. "Maybe we loosened it the first time."

Olivia, standing behind me, snorted. "It's not a jar of pickles."

I shot her a quieting glare and put my hands on the door. "Come on, give it your all," I called.

Almost as soon as we began, the padlock sprang open, then hit the dirt with a thud. The door creaked open, the shadowy interior of the shed too dark for me to tell what was inside. "Holy freaking crap," Olivia muttered.

"Find a way to tell Owen that one of the witches in the barn was trying to stop us from opening this shed," I said.

She nodded and hurried away.

"Ava wait," Drew said when I went to open the door the rest of the way. "Let me."

I hid my amusement and stood back. Sure, he was *the law*, but he was also not magical. "If you get caught in any magical booby traps, I don't want to hear it," I teased.

He chuckled and switched on his flashlight before he leaned into me until our faces were inches apart. "Hunter, remember?" I shivered and it wasn't from the fact he was a hunter, but from the seductive edge in his voice. He put some space between us and said louder, "Wait here."

Seconds after disappearing inside, he called for me. "You need to see this. Don't touch anything."

I hurried in and gasped when I saw what his flashlight illuminated. "Is that a coin press?"

Indeed, it was. "Is it possible to melt down silver with magic?" he asked.

"Absolutely." There was nothing in the shed to indicate they'd been melting it here the human way, anyway. "It's more than possible."

"Then whoever has been leading this ring is likely also our murderer," he said darkly. "And it could be any of the people out there."

"Drew," I hissed. "It's one of the people in the barn with Owen. Only when they left were we able to open this shed."

He nodded. "Any way to tell?"

I shook my head. "No, and we're still days away from having a truth serum."

"Okay. Get everyone out of here. We'll comb the place for fingerprints. I'll call you in the morning." As I turned to step outside, He grabbed my hand and pulled me to him. I stumbled then gasped as he claimed my mouth. When he broke the kiss, much too soon for my liking, he said, "Be careful."

"I will." I stood on my toes and gave him another quick kiss on the lips, then darted out of the shed.

Outside, I met Olivia's stare. She pinched the

sleeve of my shirt and tugged. "Did you two make out in the shed?"

"What? No!" My cheeks colored and I struggled to not giggle like a third-grader. "Who do you think I am?

She opened her mouth, and I held up my hand. "Don't answer that." Sucking in a deep breath, I calmed myself. Even though I was so nervous I was giggly, this wasn't a happy chore.

Turning to the witches, I lied. "It was empty except for a few old tools. If there was once something here, it's gone. Sorry I wasted your time."

A few of them muttered as they got back in the vehicle they'd ridden in on the way out here. Bevan glared as he walked to his SUV. I glared back and added a smirk for good measure.

I was sure someone would mention that we got the shed open. In fact, I was counting on it. It'd make the killer nervous knowing that I knew the fighting ring and the murders were connected. Nervous criminals made mistakes.

So, I'd let whoever-it-was sweat it out until the truth serum was ready. Then we could have a little show-and-tell party.

After the coven left, Drew replaced the padlock with one of his own and Owen spelled it surreptitiously while I announced, "I'm coming back here tomorrow to work on bringing the dead shifters to me and then getting them to their families."

Drew walked me to my car and opened the door for me. Then he caged me in with his arms against the hood. "Should I come over?"

The corners of my lips lifted. "Should you?"

Wickedness flashed in his eyes. Even though we weren't at the point in our relationship to have sex, I wasn't totally against the thought. But I did want to take it slow. Something was still holding me back.

He cupped my chin and lifted it. "What are you thinking?"

I crinkled my nose. "Overthinking. Again. Are we moving too fast?"

"I don't think so. Do you?"

I shook my head but said, "Yes...I don't know."

"I told you I want exclusive, and since we've been on three dates, it's time to make it public that we're dating." There was that seductive edginess I'd caught before. I knew from the first time I met Drew he was the alpha male type. I guessed he'd been giving me some time. And my time to decide was up.

"We're a couple, huh?"

He pressed his body into mine and dipped his head until his lips brushed my ear. "Definitely. I don't want any other man thinking you're available or anything."

Yep, the alpha male had woken. And I liked it.

I threw my arms around his neck. "I might embarrass you from time to time. Like going up to the station and staking my claim on you." I nipped at his ear. "I don't want any other woman thinking you're available."

He chuckled and pulled back a little. "I look forward to it."

CHAPTER TWENTY-THREE

*a*s promised, *way too early* the next morning, Owen and I began our work. I was working on my third cup of coffee as Olivia had shown up before it was even light outside with a large thermos of coffee and a sleepy Sam in tow.

"Come on," she said. "We can't help with the kids, but we can help keep you hydrated. I've got a cooler in the car."

Alfred ran out as we exited the house with a big plastic bag. I peeked inside. "Sandwiches?"

Grunt.

"Thank you, Alfie. You take good care of me." I touched his hand and instantly had a flash of a familiar scent. But it was gone as fast as it appeared.

I shook off the feeling the memory, or whatever it

was, stirring deep in my core. Waving at Alfred, I climbed in one of the county's police SUVs with Drew. Olivia and Sam took her 4-Runner, and we were off.

Drew and I rode to the cursed site in solemn silence. Today was going to be somber work and neither of us looked forward to it. When we pulled up beside the barn, Drew reached over and held my hand and gave it a little squeeze.

I smiled at him. "I'm dreading this, but the families need to put their kids to rest properly."

He kissed my forehead. "You got this."

His faith in me touched a deep place in my soul that I didn't think anyone, except for Clay, ever had. Maybe it was time to move on. Keep my promise to Clay that I'd live and find love again.

And I'd think harder about that subject another time. Today, I needed to raise the dead and send them home.

I had Dana and Rick along with Jennifer-Nicole's parents put the word out to any shifters who had a child go missing to meet us out here. But not until after I raised the kids from the ground. I didn't want any parent to see their kids as animated corpses

"Okay," Owen said as he sat down in the folding chair Sam pulled out of the back of the SUV. "I'm not as strong as you are, so I'm going to go in the direction of town. It seems less likely there would be any bodies out that way, or at least not as many."

"Good thinking," I said sitting in another chair a few feet from him. "I'll go toward the coast and then along the woods that stretch away from town." There was a large span of forest and mountains surrounding Shipton Harbor.

We sat and focused. Almost immediately, I began to feel them. Now that I'd done so many animals back near my house, I could tell the difference right away. I left the pure animals to their rest and only called to the shifters.

"They're coming," I whispered. A mountain of emotions swirled inside me.

Not long after the first bodies walked or crawled to us, Alissa turned up in her minivan. Several of the coven members poured out, including Bevan. "We're here to help," she said.

I'd called the coven too and asked them to come, but I wasn't hopeful they'd show. Of course, the killer would be curious, but the whole coven?

"Thank you," Olivia replied. I was too deeply focused on finding bodies to even welcome them. "I think the plan is once they get all the bodies here, we'll get them to shift and tell us who their families are. So if you could grab a notebook and pen and help me write down their information, that would be great. Once they're all raised, I'll send a text to our shifter connection."

"Where is the hunter sheriff?" someone asked. I almost laughed and broke my focus.

"He left so that he doesn't have to feel obligated to report the murders. The shifters wouldn't want their children listed in some human database, and in fact, many of these children likely don't exist on paper," Sam said then added, "For the record, I'm not here as a cop, so I don't count." I tried to tune them out as they kept talking and finally succeeded.

I stretched my net far and wide and found shifted animal after shifted animal.

Some were old. Very old. My stomach churned and my heart broke. So many kids.

Eventually, as my net widened nearly to the next town down the coast, I ran out of dead shifters to call. And as we waited on them all to come, we began the heartbreaking work of cataloging the names of the dead.

The witches quickly learned how to have the children shift from animal to human form as Owen and I animated them. Olivia and several of the coven members wrote their information down on a piece of paper and pinned it to their little bodies when they told us their details.

A couple of them looked twice at Magnus, but not enough for me to try to blame anything on him.

As they shifted back into their little bodies, Sam carefully and reverently put them in black canvas bags, then moved the location information to the outside.

I sent a text to Dana to let her know it was okay for the shifter families to come. I knew they were close by, waiting for the word.

Finally, well into the evening, all the bodies had been claimed by their parents or friend of the family. The sense of closure was there, but there was also a lot of sadness and anger. I couldn't feel any more bodies coming our way, and none of the children had been able to identify anyone other than Penny.

"It certainly seems like Penny was a major factor in all of this," I said with a sigh once all the shifters had left. I turned my gaze onto Bevan. "What do you think, Magnus?"

He looked from me to Sam and back. "How would I know?"

I shrugged. "You seem shrewd. I thought you might've drawn some conclusions."

He gasped, then snapped his mouth shut. "I haven't."

Guilty much? But the sucky part about the whole thing was we couldn't hold Bevan or anyone without proof they were involved. The truth would soon be revealed. There wasn't much we could do but wait until the serum matured.

Just as Drew pulled back up next to the barn in the same SUV he'd dropped me off in, I heard sobbing. Soft, female cries. I glanced at Olivia, who obviously heard it too. Had we missed one?

I followed the sound behind the shed where I stopped dead in my tracks. Sitting against the shed with her legs pulled to her chest and her head rested on the tops of her knees, was a small person. She looked to be around fifteen to sixteen years old, but my magic and intuition said she was older than that.

Glancing over my shoulder, I noticed that Olivia, Drew, Owen, and Sam had followed me. Dana and Rick stood back a little further. Olivia motioned for me to talk to the girl. I rolled my eyes and knelt in front of her, leaving a few feet of space between us. I needed reaction time in case she attacked me. She didn't look like she'd been dead long, but ghouls could be extremely unpredictable.

"Hello," I said softly.

She sniffed and lifted her head. Yellow cat eyes searched me. It took me off guard at first, but I managed to not gasp or jerk back. I was just too tired to freak out. Plus, enough crazy crap had happened in the last several months that I was over being shocked that another undead thing had entered my life.

She glanced behind me and shrank away. "Don't send me back."

Oh, no. "You mean back to the dead?"

She nodded. "I want to stay."

I caught Owen's attention and he shrugged. "It's up to you." Then to the girl, he said, "You do understand that you would be under Ava's protection and control. If you go rogue or turn on anyone, she will send you back with a single thought."

Wow, I could do that? Owen would know since he was my necromancer trainer. I was more powerful, but he was more knowledgeable.

The girl sat up a little straightened. "I understand. She is my Alpha. Got it. And I'll be good."

I sat on my ass in the grass next to her because my legs were starting to go numb from squatting. "What's your name?"

"Zoey."

"No last name? Do you have a family we can contact?"

Her bottom lips trembled, and she shook her head. "No. My parents died when I was young, and I've been on my own since. I didn't know where to go. I'm a tiger shifter so my cat helped me survive on my own." She ducked her head. "Or it did, I mean."

Olivia moved closer and knelt, then fell on her butt and rolled to her side. I laughed at her. "Graceful much?"

Zoey snickered as Olivia threw a handful of grass at me, then studied the girl. "She looks human. I mean, of course, she does, but she doesn't look like Alfred at all. Zoey could go out in public with a little makeup and no one would be the wiser."

My bestie was right. The girl's skin was smooth and pale, not at all like the leathery zombie-like texture of Alfred's skin. Except for the yellow cat eyes, Zoey looked like any other young adult in Shipton.

I rolled to the side and stood, making a quick decision before offering my hand to Zoey. "You'll be staying with me. I'll have to move Wallie into my office so you can have your own room. And we need to give you a last name." I thought about it for a few and said, "Lowe. That's my maiden name. My dad was a necromancer, and it would be easy enough to say you're a long-lost cousin."

Sam snorted. "A cousin who can shift into a tiger."

I waved him off and pulled the girl to a stand. She was only a couple of inches shorter than me. "Semantics." We started walking to Drew's SUV, but I stopped and turned to Zoey. "How old are you?"

"Eighteen, I think. I might be off a year or two, but I'm pretty sure it's eighteen." She glanced from me to the others as if unsure.

I started walking again. "Sounds good to me. let's go home. I'm exhausted."

CHAPTER TWENTY-FOUR

Saturday night, the truth serum was ready. We would finally be able to find out who cursed their fellow witches into accidental deaths. So I stayed up late sending letters to all the coven members to invite them over to my house for an informal meet and greet the following afternoon.

Sunday morning Drew, Sam, Olivia, Owen, and I sat down and made a plan and got everything prepared for the guests to arrive.

The coven arrived at noon. Owen and I made sure to be late. Around five after twelve, we came hurrying out of the woods. "I'm so sorry," I called, scanning the people on my porch and thrilled to find every living coven member had arrived.

Nobody wanted to miss the news about the

shifters, which was my little hook to get them there. Especially the killer who would come if it was just a social gathering. Besides, the guilty party likely figured we'd gotten it wrong since we hadn't arrested anyone or accused anyone thus far.

And thus the desperate need for information.

"Please, come in." I opened the door to find Alfred and Larry waiting expectantly, each holding a tray of drinks. Zoey sat in an oversized bean bag close to the fireplace reading a book. I motioned to her. "This is Zoey, my cousin on my dad's side of the family."

She gave them a small wave as Snooze stalked into the room and climbed on the bean bag with her, flopping down in her lap.

Several of the members nodded to her. She was good at keeping her gaze down enough to seem like she was looking at you without you noticing her cat eyes unless you stared at her long enough. Which Bevan did.

I stepped in front of Bevan, cutting off his line of sight. "Sit, drink, and give us just a minute to freshen up and we'll be right down." It was the same thing we'd done last time, but this time we'd carefully planned it.

We rushed upstairs and peeked down at the

crowd as they settled into chairs, taking sandwiches and glasses of tea, water, or lemonade from Alfred. "We have to give them time to drink," I whispered.

A few minutes later, Owen nodded. "I think they've all had at least a sip," he said. "One drop is all it takes."

"Let's go."

We headed downstairs and stood at the living room door. "Thanks again for coming. I thought you all deserved to be apprised of the situation."

Everyone's attention was on me, all of them quiet, all of them expectant.

"Now," I said and clapped my hands together. It was Drew and Sam's signal to bring Penny out.

Everyone gasped as they walked from the kitchen, where they'd been waiting just out of sight, with the spelled Penny between them. We'd put a bubble around her before we left so that nobody outside the ward could hear her at all.

"Penny, please, sit." I motioned for the only remaining chair in the room. "Have a glass of tea."

I'd warned Drew not to let her have anything to eat or drink this morning. So she was thirsty.

She gulped down a glass of tea as she perched nervously on the end of the chair.

"Lovely," I said. The coven stared at Penny with

mixed reactions of horror, suspicion, and sympathy. "Everyone, your attention here, please. Would anyone that had anything at all to do with the shifter fighting ring please stand?"

Most of the coven just looked startled, but immediately, Penny and Bevan Magnus rose to their feet. As did Melody Gonzales and Cade Duran, two of the quieter, more reserved coven members. I hadn't gotten a read on them either way before now.

Owen and I activated the ward waiting for us. Anyone who had guilt in their heart and had drunk our potion, which had combined truth serum with the guilt potion wouldn't be able to leave.

"If anyone else has any knowledge at all of the shifter fighting rings, something you knew before we broke this open, please stand."

Joely Travis stood.

"Wow," Olivia whispered. "That's insane."

"Indeed," Drew said. "Everyone else, please head to your homes. Thank you for your help."

"It's all her fault," Bevan cried, pointing to Penny. "She's a psychopath!"

"Which of you is the murderer?" I asked.

Bevan slammed his lips shut and his face began to turn colors. First pink, then red, then purple. Sinking into his chair, he began to sob. "She's my sister," he gasped. "She's been running the shifter ring. She ran it with her husband."

I gasped, staring at Penny. "Is this true?" I couldn't imagine her and Billy being this devious.

She hung her head but didn't answer.

"What about the murders?" I asked. I had to be the one to ask the questions since I'd brewed the potion.

Bevan moaned, ran his chubby hand through his brown hair, and finally, he spoke again. "It's me," he whispered. "Billy figured it out. I was getting rid of anyone who crossed me, and he bound my ability to take a life for years... decades. I don't know where he got a spell like that, but I couldn't kill anyone. But when he died, it all came back to me." He grunted, trying hard to fight the compulsion to tell the truth. "All my power, unrestricted."

I moved back a few steps as his face twisted in a perverse pleasure. His brown eyes darkened.

"My mother?" I whispered.

He stopped grinning and looked me in the eye. The room went quiet as Bevan sucked in a deep breath. "Your mother found out I was Penny's brother. She kept sticking her damn nose in where it wasn't wanted." A little piece of spittle flew from his mouth.

Fury raced through my blood, hot and ready to zap the snot out of him. Magic I didn't know I possessed pooled in the palms of my hand. Drew stepped up behind me, placed his hands on my shoulders, and whispered, "He's not worth wasting your magic on."

He was right. Leaning back against him, I calmed my emotions as the truth settled in.

Bevan killed my mom. Stole her from me. The magic tingled my fingers, ready to unleash. Just then, Drew kissed my temple and the raging current settled down. A little.

"The coin was all too easy to slip into her pocket. After that, I just had to wait for the curse to do its job. A lightning strike?" He laughed, the deep sound pounding against my eardrums, freaking me out since he didn't actually smile or look away from me. "Hers was a particularly..." he paused and sucked in a deep breath. "*Delicious* kill."

Drew stepped around me, but I held my hand up to stop him. I had a grip on my magic now. Walking toward the man who killed my mother, I bent in front of him and leaned forward, not at all scared he might hurt me. I whispered words only for the murderer. "I hope you live a *long* time in prison,

Magnus. Because the moment you die, you will belong to me."

As I pulled back, I finally saw a glimpse of fear in the psychopath's eyes. "Burn his witch's mark before you take him to jail," I said. "He won't be able to practice magic with a scar over it."

As a hunter, Drew knew all too well what I meant and probably already knew how to do it.

I put my hand on Drew's arm. "Burn it deep."

"I know," Drew murmured. "I will."

Walking out of the living room, I headed straight for the back door, went down the patio steps, and kept walking until I couldn't go any farther.

I sat down at the edge of the cliff, looking out over the ocean. Tears rolled down my cheeks and my chest tightened. Memories of the day she died filled my mind. The lightning, her falling. Me desperately trying to heal her with my magic.

I now realized it hadn't been my failure as a necromancer or my inexperience. It was the curse that had kept me from healing or raising her. Magnus must have added that into her curse so she couldn't be brought back.

"Mom." My voice broke. I didn't know what to say. I wasn't sure if she could even hear me.

"Ava?"

The familiar voice startled me. I turned to see my mom standing a few feet behind me. "Mom? How are you here?"

Her sea-green eyes, just like mine, twinkled. "You called me." She tossed her blonde hair, unlike mine, over her shoulder. I'd forgotten how svelte she was. I didn't get that from her either. I was curvy, to say the least.

I'd called her? I had no clue I could talk to a ghost. Wait. "Are you a ghoul?"

She laughed and shook her head. "No, I'm a ghost."

There was something in her voice that set off warning bells. "Mom, are you okay?"

She looked around like she wasn't sure where she was then focused on me. "Thank you for setting the children free." She looked around. "I have to go." Then she vanished.

I ran forward. "Mom!"

But she was gone. I dropped to sit on the ground, feeling defeated and inspired at the same time. I'd talked to a ghost. My mom's ghost. I could do it again. And I would figure it out one way or another.

"Ava!" Drew yelled. "I need you to come in here!"

I turned from the cliff, wiping my eyes. Drew stood on the porch frantically gesturing. "Now!"

Okay, Mr. Bossy Alpha Man.

Running as fast as I could, I crossed grass-covered ground, watching where I was going so I didn't faceplant. I wasn't as coordinated as I once was. Not that I was ever terribly coordinated.

I hadn't learned much defensive magic yet, outside of calling for dead things to aid me. I gathered my power as I vaulted up the porch steps. There was a field full of dead animals that I could call to help us if Bevan had managed to do something Owen and the non-witches couldn't handle.

But when I thundered into the living room, prepared to release a huge burst of necromancy magic, Luci sat on my couch with his feet propped up. "Lovely of you to join us," he said as he bit into a shiny red apple.

Gasping, I let the power go and leaned forward with my hands on my knees. Bevan and Penny had been bound by magical ropes, by the feel of it.

Relief spread all through me, and my adrenaline dropped. Heaving, I hung my head and stood bent over in the middle of my living room, desperately trying to catch my breath.

Mortified that Drew was seeing me so out of

breath after one small sprint, I righted myself and bit back my heaving breaths.

But that made black spots appear in my eyes. I gulped in a deep breath as slowly as I could, praying it wouldn't look like I was still winded from that small bit of exertion.

Damn it. I was getting a treadmill desk, pronto.

"What are you doing here?" I asked. "I thought I'd made you mad so you'd abandoned me."

Lucifer waved his hand. "Don't be silly. I've never abandoned you. It was apparent you wanted to do things your way, so I let you. I've been watching, don't worry."

Crossing my arms, I glared at the devil. "If you've been aware of all this, why did you allow these people to be killed?" I asked in a near-yell. My emotions went back to running rogue from everything that had happened.

Luci stood and sucked in a deep breath. "Oh, yeah, see there are rules. Strict edicts I must obey. But if you'll notice, since the moment I began to suspect who our culprit was, there haven't been any more murders." He winked at me.

Bevan's head swung around. "You? You were the one who kept me from getting a coin into Ava's pocket?"

Me? I glared at Bevan. "I can't wait for you to die," I whispered, and this time, everyone heard me.

"Well, my dear, I watched you all right." Luci tapped my nose. "I'm very impressed. Whenever you're ready, I've got a few managerial positions I desperately need to fill in Hell."

I gulped and looked around for any of my friends to help.

The cowards. They all stood back and blanched when I turned to them for help. "Thanks," I said shakily. Then I held up my hand to him. "Not today, Satan. Or, you know, ever."

"If all the fun is over, I'll just..." He turned to Penny and Bevan, then snapped his fingers.

With a sound like a roaring campfire, they disappeared, leaving a black scorch mark on my floor. "Perfect," Luci said. He turned and clasped his hands. "You don't have any more of that stew, do you?"

Alfred grunted behind me, and I slowly turned my head, then my body, as I watched Lucifer follow the ghoul into the kitchen.

When I fully turned, I caught sight of all the shocked expressions behind me.

"Well," Drew said. "That's one way to do it."

CHAPTER TWENTY-FIVE

TWO WEEKS LATER

"*T*hank you all for coming to our new and improved coven meeting." I stood in my living room and beamed at the full house.

After a huge debate and a lot of begging—mostly me pleading with the coven that I wasn't leader material—I caved and drank the High Witch potion. I was their leader now, and as such, I made a few changes. Which explained my full house.

Olivia had to bring chairs from her house, and Drew had even dropped off a few camp chairs. But we had enough. Alfred had been cooking all week. Larry was thrilled he didn't have to hide from the guests. He'd decided he wanted to stay with me because I kept things interesting. His words.

And my *cousin*, Zoey, was thrilled to meet so many magical people her age. But we kept the little fact that she was undead to our small inner circle and the magical dozen, the natural-born witches who were honest and strong enough to pass my tests.

Owen had helped me figure out what to look for when selecting the twelve witches who would back me when high magic and planning were needed. I considered them to be my board and advisers.

"Our new coven is all-inclusive. We welcome all walks of witches as well as the humans who know about us and might need some witchy support. Sitting on either side of me were my magical dozen, the officers and board members of the coven. If you have an issue or questions you can go to any of them."

Olivia stood and held up a hand. "Please, humans, fill out the sign-up sheet for the Not a Sup Support Group, or NAS for short." She pointed toward the foyer where we had a table set up with reading material and the NAS sign-up sheet. "We're going to meet once a month at my place."

She was in her element, absolutely thrilled to be a part of this. Sam stood back, a little overwhelmed as he looked at his life-long neighbors that he'd never known were magical.

"Now, for our first coven meeting, we have very special guests." I clasped my hands in front of me. "Please welcome Ricky and Dana Johnson."

Everyone knew what they'd been through, losing a son and then almost losing another. When they stood and waved, the entire group clapped, and slowly, everyone got to their feet as Dana buried her face in Ricky's chest and sobbed.

I held one hand up and everyone sat back down. "Rick and Dana have graciously agreed to be our liaison with the shifters, which is something we've needed for a very long time." I addressed the couple directly. "You're always welcome in this coven, and if you ever have a need for a friend, you know where to find a bunch."

"Thank you," Dana mouthed as they took their seats.

Alfred grunted in the doorway, and I looked over to see he had his tuxedo apron on, and he nodded sharply at me when he caught my eye. "I'm being told dinner is ready. Please, enjoy."

I stepped back as everyone got to their feet, nodding at my coven. All the witches who hadn't been involved with the shifters and the murders had readily agreed to join the new, improved coven.

Alfred stood back with Larry, who had flat refused to be laid to rest. The ghoul grunted something to the skeleton and Larry ran over to the counter, grabbed a stack of napkins, and wedged himself between the people lined up on either side of my table to make a plate of the bountiful feast.

Larry brushed up against the twins, having darted between them, and they both jerked back with mirroring faces of horror at having a skeleton touching them.

I put my hand on my mouth and bit back a giggle. I had warned everyone about my menagerie beforehand.

"Now."

Jerking around, I looked behind me for the person who dared speak to me like that. But nobody was behind me.

"Now."

What the fudge? I looked in a circle, then Snoozer rubbed against my legs. When I looked down at him, he looked up at me with his big smoochy face. "Meow."

"Geez, Snoozle," I said, bending to scoop him up into my arms. "I thought you said now."

As if on cue, his stomach gurgled. "Oh, it's your dinner time, isn't it?"

"Now."

I stopped and stared into his too-intelligent eyes. "If you're going to start talking, I'm packing up and moving back to Philadelphia, cause that's the straw that broke the camel's back.

"Meow."

"That's better."

I handed him off to Alfred. "He's hungry."

Alfie grunted, then glared at Snoozle. "Now," Snooze said.

"And demanding," I added.

A couple of the coven members' kids ran by, closely pursued by Sammie, who was having the time of his life.

"Uncle Drew is here!" he screeched as he ran onto the back porch.

Owen and I had made a big bubble for the backyard so that we could all go out back and enjoy the weather without being cold. I laughed at the kids and moved toward the front door to greet Drew.

But when I opened it, he was quickly walking back down my front walk. "Drew?" I asked.

We'd had one more date since the day Luci took the murdering Bevan and Penny to Hell. We'd been spending a lot of time together since we spent the entire day at the festival, just the two of us laughing and goofing off.

And it had gone very, very well.

He turned slowly and squinted at me. "I forgot."

Cocking my head, I walked down the porch steps and met him halfway up my walk. "Forgot what?"

"That you were having your big meeting tonight. I'm sorry."

"Why are you sorry?"

"It's one thing to give up a life of hunting, but that?" He shook his head rapidly. "I can't be closed up in a house with that many witches. It makes my skin tingle." He gestured to all the cars parked along my yard and driveway. "As soon as I pulled in, I figured out what was going on, but I wanted to come to say hi anyway."

"And then?"

"When I got close, I got itchy. I had to back away from the house quickly."

I laughed and grabbed his hand. "How about a kiss for the road and you come to dinner tomorrow night?"

A sexy smile lifted the corners of his mouth and he wrapped his arms around my waist, jerking me close. I sighed as he claimed my lips like he was starving. Pressing into him, I deepened the kiss. My body tingled all over and ached in all the right places.

The chime of my phone broke us apart. I pulled it out of my pocket and drew my brows together as I read the text.

"What is it?" Drew leaned over to read my text.

"That's Uncle Wade, Clay's uncle. He said the realtor has a buyer for the house and she wants to meet with me next weekend." While I was thrilled that the house sold, it also meant one more thing to let go of. My entire life with Clay had been in the house.

Drew cupped my chin and lifted. "Are you okay?"

I nodded and pocketed my phone. "Yeah. I am." He raised his brows. "Honestly, I'll be fine. It'll be rough letting go of the last thing I have of Clay's, but it'll be okay."

Drew kissed me softly on the lips. "Not the last thing. You have Wallie and your memories and your love. Clay will always be in your heart."

How did I luck out with such a compassionate, understanding man? Twice.

"I'll be going with you."

"What? No. You can't—"

He kissed me again to cut off my words, then

said, "I'm going and Wallie will go. You're not doing this alone."

The man I was lucky to find was also bossy and completely wonderful. "Thank you."

"No need to thank me." He gave me one more kiss before stepping back. "You better get back to your party."

"See you tomorrow."

He gave me a wicked grin and turned toward his car. I took a few minutes to enjoy the view. After he drove off, I sent Wallie a text.

House has a buyer. You need to come with me to meet them next weekend.

His reply was instant. **Sure meet you there? Yep**.

Another chapter in my life was about to end. When I looked at my new family and the coven I was rebuilding and the new beau in my life, I knew everything was going to be okay.

Clay would be proud of me.

SNEAK PEEK INTO A NEW SERIES
COMING SOON

A bunny bit me on the finger and everything went sideways after that.

That's just the beginning of my insane life. The Fascinators, the local ladies' club, suddenly are incredibly interested in having me join their next Bunco night, which is a thinly veiled excuse to drink and gossip.

I've been dying to get into that group for years; why now? I'm over forty, my daughter is grown, and all I do is temp work. What's so special about me?

After I shift into a dragon, things become clearer. They're not a Bunco group. The Fascinators are a pack of shifters. Yes, shifters. Like werewolves, except in this case it's weresquirrels and a wereskunk, among others.

And my daughter? She wants to move home, suddenly and suspiciously. As excited as I am to have her home, why? She loves being on her own. It's got something to do with a rough pack of predators, shifters who want to watch the world burn. I hope she's not mixed up with the wrong crowd.

There's also a mysterious mountain man hanging around out of the blue. Where was he before the strange bunny bite? Nowhere near me, that's for sure.

Life is anything but boring. At this point, I'm just hoping that I'll survive it all with my tail—literally —intact.

Preorder your copy today

WITCHING AFTER FORTY SERIES

Witching After Forty follows the misadventures of Ava Harper – a forty-something necromancer with a light witchy side that you wouldn't expect from someone who can raise the dead. Join Ava as she learns how to start over after losing the love of her life, in this new paranormal women's fiction series with a touch of cozy mystery, magic, and a whole lot of mayhem.

A Ghoulish Midlife
Cookies for Satan (Christmas novella)
I'm With Cupid (Valentine novella)
A Cursed Midlife
Feeding Them Won't Make Them Grow (Novella in the Charity Anthology, Eat Your Heart Out)

A Girlfriend For Mr. Snoozerton (Novella)

A Haunting Midlife

An Animated Midlife

A Killer Midlife

More coming soon

ABOUT LIA DAVIS

Lia Davis is the USA Today bestselling author of more than forty books, including her fan favorite Shifter of Ashwood Falls Series.

A lifelong fan of magic, mystery, romance and adventure, Lia's novels feature compassionate alpha heroes and strong leading ladies, plenty of heat, and happily-ever-afters.

Lia makes her home in Northeast Florida where she battles hurricanes and humidity like one of her heroines.

When she's not writing, she loves to spend time with her family, travel, read, enjoy nature, and spoil her kitties.

She also loves to hear from her readers. Send her a note at lia@authorliadavis.com!

Follow Lia on Social Media

Website: http://www.authorliadavis.com/

Newsletter: http://www.
subscribepage.com/authorliadavis.newsletter
Facebook author fan page: https://www.
facebook.com/novelsbylia/
Facebook Fan Club: https://www.facebook.com/
groups/LiaDavisFanClub/
Twitter: https://twitter.com/novelsbylia
Instagram: https://www.
instagram.com/authorliadavis/
BookBub: https://www.bookbub.com/authors/lia-
davis
Pinterest: http://www.pinterest.com/liadavis35/
Goodreads: http://www.goodreads.com/author/
show/5829989.Lia_Davis

Marked by Darkness

His Big Bad Wolf (MM)

Their Royal Ash

Tempting the Wolf

Hexed with Sass (part of the Milly Taiden Sassy Ever After World)

Claiming Her Dragons (Part of the Milly Taiden Paranormal Dating Agency)

Contemporaries

Pleasures of the Heart Series

Single Titles

His Guarded Heart (MM)

L.A. (Lainie) Boruff lives in East Tennessee with her husband, three children, and an ever-growing number of cats. She loves reading, watching TV, and procrastinating by browsing Facebook. L.A.'s passions include vampires, food, and listening to heavy metal music. She once won a Harry Potter trivia contest based on the books and lost one based on the movies. She has two bands on her bucket list that she still hasn't seen: AC/DC and Alice Cooper. Feel free to send tickets.

L.A.'s Facebook Group: https://www.facebook.com/groups/LABoruffCrew/

Follow L.A. on Bookbub if you like to know

about new releases but don't like to be spammed:
https://www.bookbub.com/profile/l-a-boruff

The Unseen War

Paranormal Reverse Harem

War of Fangs

War of Fire

War of Wings

Coven's End

Complete Paranormal Reverse Harem co-write with Lia Davis

Kane

Voss

Quin

Jillian

Coven's End: The Complete Series Boxed Set

Academy's Rise

Paranormal Reverse Harem co-write with Lia Davis

Hell Fire

Dark Water

Dead Air

Academy's Rise: The Complete Series Boxed Set

Valentine Pride

Complete Paranormal Reverse Harem co-write with Laura Greenwood

Unicorn Mates

Unicorn Luck

Unicorn Truth

A Platypus and Her Mates

The Firehouse Feline

Paranormal Comedic Reverse harem co-write with Laura Greenwood and Lacey Carter Andersen

Feline the Heat

Feline the Flames

Feline the Pressure

Magic & Metaphysics Academy

Paranormal Academy Reverse Harem co-write with Laura Greenwood

Magical Mischief

Magical Mistake

Magical Misfit

Southern Soil

Sweet Contemporary Reverse Harem

Literary Yours

Snow Cure

Made in the USA
Middletown, DE
20 March 2021